DEVIL'S ROAD

MATT GAMBLE THRILLER SERIES BOOK 2

GARY WINSTON BROWN

This is a work of fiction. Names, characters, places, and incidents – and their usage for storytelling purposes – are crafted for the singular purpose of fictional entertainment and no absolute truths shall be derived from the information contained within. Locales, businesses, companies, events, government institutions, law enforcement agencies and private or educational institutions are used for atmospheric, entertainment and fictional purposes only. Furthermore, any resemblance or reference to persons living or dead is used fictitiously for atmospheric, entertainment and fictional purposes.

Cover design: Taherul

Image credit: Freepix, Depositphotos

❀ Created with Vellum

This book is dedicated to my beautiful wife, Fiona.
I'm lucky to have you in my life and in my corner.

ILYBBOBKS...ATS

1

Tell Me What You Know

C ENTRAL INTELLIGENCE AGENCY
Langley, Virginia

TASK FORCE CHIEF Cameron Cross heard the knock on his door. His response was gruff, as though the interruption was unexpected, which it was not. "Come," he said.

Director Ferriman entered the room and found his boss standing in the middle of his office, staring at a television monitor on his wall, watching the news. A ticker scrolled across the bottom of the screen, providing updates on the story of the massive explosion that had awakened the sleeping residents of a quiet New York City suburb around midnight, taking half of the waterfront business district with it when it went up in flames.

Cross kept watching the screen as he pointed. "Sit."

Ferriman sat in a guest chair. He had a sinking feeling the meeting would be the shortest of his career.

Cross's eyes never left the screen as he spoke. "You know how long I've been in this job?" he asked.

Ferriman knew better than to answer. The question didn't require one. He waited.

"Too fucking long," Cross continued. "You know what comes with that?"

This required an answer. "No, sir."

"After a while, you develop a sixth sense for things. It's like there's no secret the world can keep from you anymore, no bullshit you can't smell from a thousand miles away. You can tell what is and isn't an agency op." He pointed to the screen. "And this clusterfuck has our DNA all over it." He turned and faced his subordinate. "Tell me I'm wrong."

Ferriman shook his head.

"Jesus. Was this Gamble?"

"I believe so, sir."

"You *believe* so. That implies you're not sure."

"Intel is still coming in. We have people at the scene. They've confirmed that the asset who had been assigned to take out Gamble is dead."

"What about Reese?"

"We assume she's with him."

Cross turned off the monitor, returned to his desk, sat in his chair. "Tell me what you know."

"Badger was the primary asset assigned to locate Gamble. I received a call from him last night. He informed me that the capture/kill order had been fulfilled with terminal results and that both Gamble and Reese were dead. As it turns out, even though the call had originated from his encrypted phone, it had been faked."

"How the hell is that possible?"

"I believe that either Gamble or Reese took him out, used his biometrics to unlock the phone, then called me. I'm not familiar with Badger's voice, so I had no idea it wasn't him I was speaking to."

"Who was it?"

"I don't know. Communications was able to identify the last known location of Badger's phone. I'm sure you can guess where that was."

"The site of the explosion."

Ferriman nodded.

"What do we know now?"

"I've dispatched an agent to poke around the area and find out what he can without showing our hand to the local authorities." The text alert on Ferriman's phone sounded. He read the message. "That's him. He's been able to tie into NYPD comms. One of their helicopter's reports seeing a body in tactical gear on the rooftop of an adjoining building. FLiR indicates there's no heat signature. They're deploying a SWAT team to check it out. The chopper also reports seeing shell casings around the body and a vehicle parked on the street, possibly belonging to the shooter."

"That's Badger. He must have tried to take out Gamble and Reese from the rooftop."

"So it seems."

"Where do we go from here?" Cross asked. "As soon as Badger's body reaches the morgue, the medical examiner is going to take his prints and hand them over to the NYPD, who'll soon realize he doesn't officially exist. Once that happens, they'll know that whatever went down there is way above their pay grade. They'll start asking questions. It'll go up the chain. Sooner or later, it'll hit my desk. And you know how much I hate hearing my phone ring."

"I do, sir," Ferriman answered.

"Good. Tell your agent to pull video footage from the area up to and including the moment of the blast. Have him access everything he can from surrounding businesses, residential door cams, police observation devices, the works. Gamble might be good, but he's not that good. He can't disappear into thin air. He left a trail. You need to find it."

"Yes, sir."

Ferriman's phone sounded once more. He read the text.

"What is it?" Cross asked.

"NYPD crime scene techs found the remains of a fire-bombed vehicle behind the building. It contained a cache of weapons. They also found traces of a liquid accelerant and parts of a remote ignition system, the type used by professionals to set off pyrotechnic displays from a safe distance. Similar ignitors were found throughout the building. This explosion was no accident. It was deliberate. Someone blew up the place for a reason."

"Gamble and Reese."

Ferriman nodded. "Has to be."

"But why?"

Ferriman rose from his chair. "I don't know. But I plan to find out."

4

Rendezvous

C ARGO VESSEL GOLIATH
22 days at sea
19:30 hours CST

Latitude: 16.003575733881327

Longitude: -82.924804687500001

12 nautical miles off the coast of Puerto Lempira, Honduras

MATT AND KYLA stood on the freighter's starboard deck and watched as the go-fast boat raced across the water, approached the ship, then pulled alongside the vessel, matched its speed. Captain Alvarez stood beside them, waiting for his crew members to lower the switchback gangway and deploy the rope ladder. Below, the Cigarette jet boat turned off its running lights. Its powerful engines gurgled as its operator matched the Goliath's speed and maintained a narrow gap between the immense ship with which it had been contracted to rendezvous. When the gangway was ready, a crew member gave the captain the thumbs up. Alvarez nodded, pointed to the watertight deck door on their left. The man spoke to his shipmates. Their task completed, they exited the deck.

From the Cigarette boat below, a flashlight beam flickered three times. The waiting boat was ready to receive its passengers.

With a wave, the captain acknowledged the craft. He turned to Matt and Kyla. "She's a fast boat," Alvarez said. "We're still in international waters, approximately twelve miles from shore. You'll be in Puerto Lempira in five minutes." He glanced down at the waiting boat. "You should know something about those boat operators, Mr. Reid. They are modern-day pirates and, therefore, unpredictable. Don't turn your back on him for a second. I assume he has already been paid for their services?"

Matt nodded. "He has."

"Don't think he won't try to demand more. I assume you have, what shall we call it, a contingency fund for use in the event of such an emergency?"

"I might."

"Good. I would be very surprised if you were not required to dip into it. Honduras is a corrupt country, and the men in that boat are as corrupt as they come." Alvarez paused, looked at Matt thoughtfully. "Might I ask what really brings you here?"

Kyla took Matt's arm in hers, replied. "We hear the beaches are great."

Alvarez smiled. "That is true. However, most tourists tend to leave their country by plane and document their arrival and departure through Customs and Immigration, not by a go-fast boat."

"I'm not one for waiting in lines," Matt said. "And have you tasted airline food recently? Terrible."

Alvarez laughed. "You have all your belongings with you?"

Matt slung his backpack over his shoulder. "I'm good."

Kyla replied. "Same."

"Then you're all set."

"I just have one concern, Captain," Matt said.

"What's that?"

"Your men."

Alvarez shook his head. "You don't have to worry about them. They have excellent-paying jobs and families who rely on them to keep them. They know better than to gossip or talk out of turn. This is not the first time they have seen executives from our shipping line arrive and depart from the Goliath in such a manner. And although you and I know that is not the truth, it is the cover story they have been told, and the one they undoubtedly believe. You've carried out the assignments I've given you while on board quite convincingly. I see no reason why anyone would suspect you to be anyone other than who you have represented yourselves to be."

Matt recalled the briefing Oleg Schroeder had conducted with him and Kyla as they left New York harbor in the wake of the explosion that had obliterated Red Thunder. He explained how he had reached out to his good friend, Captain Miguel Alvarez, agreed upon Matt and Kyla's cover story, and secured their passage aboard the Goliath on the condition that the boarding must be done while the vessel was traveling at speed. Before their boarding, Alvarez had placed a call and reached out to one of his contacts in China. Half a world away, the young man hacked into the Goliath's computer system and shut down its hundreds of video surveillance cameras for two minutes, just long enough for Matt and Kyla to disembark from the go-fast boat where it had met up with the ship off the coast of Cuba and board the Goliath. The same was being done now.

Alvarez checked his watch. "I'm afraid we can't delay your departure any longer," he said. "I must bring the cameras back online. You'll have to leave now."

Matt nodded, shook Alvarez's hand, as did Kyla. "Thank you, Captain," he said.

"Be safe, Mr. Reid... Ms. Wright," Alvarez said, addressing them by the cover names. "Remember what I said about the man in that boat."

Kyla smiled. "We will."

Matt and Kyla walked down the gangway, descended the rope ladder, jumped into the waiting go-fast boat, took their seats.

With their passengers safely aboard, the driver leaned into the throttle and powered up the Cigarette. It pulled away from the Goliath, its mighty engines accelerating to speed, and set course for Puerto Lempira.

Remembering the captain's warning, Matt placed his backpack on his lap, unzipped a side compartment, and wrapped his hand around the grip of the Sig Sauer P365 pistol hidden within it.

In five minutes, he and Kyla would be safely on Honduran soil.

Or so he hoped.

3

The Law Of The Water

ERRIMAN WAS CONCERNED. For the past three weeks, the operatives assigned to track down Matt and Kyla had come up empty. Badger's body had been recovered from a rooftop several buildings down from the now burned-out shell of Red Thunder Fireworks Manufacturing, taken to the morgue for examination, and the cause of death determined to have been murder. Attempts made to ascertain the man's identity through facial recognition software, fingerprint analysis, CODIS, NDIS, and AFDIL DNA matching programs had been met without success. That no record could be found of him anywhere only served to deepen the mystery of who he was and how he had come to be found dead atop the building, his body surrounded by spent shell casings, yet not in possession of a weapon. His termination had been attributed to two distinct penetration wounds, one extending distally down through his right shoulder into his chest cavity, the second through his lower back, severing his spinal cord. While the authorities continued investigating the matter, Ferriman's team waited for the right moment to act. One week later, workers arrived to find that the dead man's body had disappeared from the morgue. No signs of a break-in were evident. It was clear that whoever the man had worked for wanted to ensure the query into his identity stopped. While the NYPD went through the motions of investigating the matter, everyone knew that the truth would never be ascertained. Attention was quickly shifted to the discovery of the city's largest underground methamphetamine production facility found beneath Red Thunder and the man identified as the building's owner, New York real estate mogul David Forsythe. Ferriman couldn't have cared less about Forsythe. He wanted Gamble and Reese. And he wanted them now.

Ferriman heard the knock on his door. "Enter," he said.

Analyst Tonya Best entered the room, laptop in hand. "We may have a possible lead on Gamble and Reese, sir," she said.

"What is it?"

"Video footage taken by a boater in the harbor at the time of the explosion which took out the fireworks company." Best opened her computer, placed it on Ferriman's desk, played the video file, and waited for his reaction.

Ferriman watched the footage, shrugged. "It's the same coverage of Red Thunder blowing up that news agencies have been broadcasting for the past three weeks. Why are you wasting my time with this? It's nothing I haven't seen before."

"On the contrary, Director," Best said. "Pay close attention to the last two seconds." She pressed the play icon in the middle of the screen. The ten-second video panned from right to left. The first few seconds captured the explosion. The next followed the fireball as it erupted from the van and rose high into the air. The last two seconds caught the image of a boat west of the videographer's position as it disappeared from frame.

"It's a boat," Ferriman said. "So what?"

Best played the video once more, commented on the footage. "There were four boats in the harbor when Red Thunder exploded," she said. "The boat belonging to the guy who shot this video, plus three others. All were heading out into the harbor. As soon as the explosion occurred, three of the boats, including this guys, immediately changed course and made a beeline straight for the blast's location. Why? Because it's the law of the water. Even though the explosion happened on land, the fireworks factory is on the waterfront. I'd bet my pension that the first thought that occurred to the captains of those boats was to get to the public launch as fast as possible and render assistance to anyone who might have escaped from the building." She touched the screen. "But this vessel... the *Off The Hook*... it didn't turn around. It kept on going. This begs the question."

Ferriman leaned back in his chair, crossed his arms. "Why didn't it follow the others to the launch to offer help?"

"Exactly," Best said. "It should have. Surely, the other boats would have expected it to join them. It was right there. The blast lit up its transom, made its name visible in the video."

"It had no intention of turning around."

Best nodded. "And I think I know why." She replayed the video, froze it at the last frame, then increased the image to full screen. Two shadowy figures stood at the transom, watching Red Thunder go up in flames.

Ferriman leaned forward, adjusted his glasses, stared intently at the screen. "Who is that?" he asked.

"My guess is it's Gamble and Reese. That's why we haven't been able to find them. We've been looking in the wrong place. They aren't stateside. They were on this boat, headed where we don't know."

"Do we know who the captain is?"

Best shook her head. "I haven't looked into that yet. I wanted to run this footage past you first and take direction from there."

"Find out," Ferriman replied. "I'll dispatch a team to locate him, then transport him to a rendition site for questioning. I want to interview him myself."

Best closed her laptop. "Yes, sir."

"This was excellent work, Tonya."

"Thank you, sir," the analyst replied, then left the director's office.

Ferriman leaned back in his chair and smiled. "Clever, Matt," he said. "Very clever."

4

The Way It Is

ATT CLUTCHED THE handgun in his backpack, his trigger finger resting on the slide as the Cigarette boat left the Goliath and planed across the calm Honduran waters. The sky was clear, the night moonless. In the distance, a faint glow danced across the treetops of a tropical rainforest. He called out to the boat's driver. "How much farther?"

"One minute," the driver replied. He pointed toward the dark shore. "That is Pusuaya. Yahurabila is just ahead. We'll enter the lagoon at Barra de Caratasca. There's a fishing dock at Puerto Lempira. From there, you're on your own. You'll need a car and driver but be warned, do not take a taxi. It's too dangerous. Gangs roam the roads in Honduras. They won't think twice about stopping the driver to identify his passengers. When they see that you are Americans, they'll take everything you have, but not before making you transfer every last cent from your bank accounts into theirs. Resist their demands, and they'll kill you on the spot. But your wife will be spared."

"Why not kill me too?" Kyla asked.

The driver smiled. "Because beautiful American women fetch a very high price here."

Kyla glanced at Matt. "Don't let me out of your sight."

Matt smiled. "I'm more worried about what you'll do to them than what they'll do to you."

Kyla nodded, opened her backpack, removed her Glock, chambered a round, slipped the weapon into her waistband in the small of her back. "Damn right."

The driver slowed the jet boat as it approached the narrow inlet, then reduced its engines to a near stop. The powerful craft putted through the waterway, entered the lagoon. Ahead, a lamp post illuminated the end of a long wooden pier. Two young children ran to meet the craft as it docked. They yelled at Matt and Kyla in Spanish as the boat's pilot tossed them a mooring line, which they quickly secured to the docking post. Matt opened his backpack, removed two candy bars, handed one to each of the children. They thanked him and ran off.

The driver smiled. "You just made their night," he said. "Most families here in Puerto Lempira earn their living from the sea. They are very poor. Chocolate is a luxury they can rarely afford."

"They're children," Matt said. "They should be able to enjoy an occasional treat."

"Better it comes from you than the gangs."

"Why?" Kyla asked.

"It's how they bait them into the life," the driver replied.

"Chocolate, toys, money, new clothes... all are tools used to seduce them. The largest gang, the Mara Salvatrucha, begins recruiting members when they are still children. By the age of seven, they've been indoctrinated into a faction. By twelve, they're carrying out murders at the request of their leaders. It's a sad state of affairs, to say the least. But here in Honduras, that's just the way it is."

"That isn't right," Kyla said. "What is your government doing about it?"

The boat pilot shrugged. "Attempts have been made to put an end to the gangs," he replied. "But it is a nearly impossible challenge. Their influence runs deep, perhaps into the halls of government itself, as many suspect. Corruption is everywhere in my country. Governmental and criminal justice system reform takes years to accomplish. The president wants to build an island prison on the Isle del Cisne archipelago, round up the gang leaders, and send them there. Whether such a project is ever undertaken remains to be seen. The people see it as political optics and not much more."

A man stood at the end of the long wharf, his image silhouetted against the row of ramshackle buildings that faced the lagoon.

Matt glanced at the boat pilot, pointed to the man. "Is he with you?"

The pilot shook his head. "That is Xiomara. He is a produce vendor here in Puerto Lempira. He meets all the boats that arrive."

"So he's what... the local welcoming committee?"

"No. Once you leave the wharf, he will offer to drive you to your destination. You would be wise to accept."

"Why would I do that?"

"Because the gangs will not stop him. They know him as a vendor, not a taxi driver. If it's a ride you need, Xiomara will provide you with safe passage wherever you want to go."

"How much?" Matt asked.

The pilot smiled. "How much is your life worth?"

Matt nodded. "Understood."

"Pay him more than he asks. You are alone here. You need every ally you can get."

Matt and Kyla exited the jet boat and stepped onto the pier. The pilot turned off the engine, joined them. "Where are you headed from here?" he asked.

"We're not sure," Matt replied.

The pilot cocked his head. "You traveled all this way with no final destination in mind? You don't strike me as the kind of man who does not follow a plan."

"I'm not."

The pilot smiled. "Ah, I understand now. The captain warned you about me, didn't he?"

"He suggested we be careful."

"As you should. But he is generalizing. It is true that there are boat pilots here who would not think twice about taking you deep into a desolate lagoon, demand everything you have, then put a bullet in your head. I am not such a man. I run a legitimate service and am paid very well for providing it. I don't consider murdering my customers good for business."

"Glad to hear it."

The pilot extended his hand. "My name is Lorenzo. Should you require my services again, ask for me. My boat is the only one of its kind in Honduras. Those who know me will know where to find me."

Matt shook his hand. "Thank you, Lorenzo."

Lorenzo removed the mooring lines from the dock posts, tossed them into the boat, stepped in, took his place at the helm, started the Cigarette. He called out above the engine's thrum as the boat pulled away from the dock. "You can trust Xiomara to take you where you need to go. Good luck to you both."

Matt and Kyla watched the jet boat leave the lagoon.

Kyla turned to Matt. "So, what's the plan?" she asked.

Matt nodded in Xiomara's direction. "We see a man about a ride."

"And after that?"

"Try not to get killed along the way."

5

Mr. Schroeder?

OLEG SCHROEDER BACKED the *Off The Hook* into its slip at the Marine Basin Marina. The 45' Custom Lohr Express sport fishing charter boat eased to a stop, then bobbed in the water. Oleg turned off the engine, secured its mooring lines, grabbed a leather satchel and FOR SALE sign from inside the cabin, locked the cabin door, hung the sign on the boat's transom railing, then left the craft and strolled along the pier to the main security gate.

The guard welcomed him as he approached. "Evening, Captain," he said. He saw Schroeder was alone. "No clients tonight?"

Oleg smiled. Like the last clandestine charter he had run nearly a month ago for his friend, Kyla Reese, tonight's run was off the books. He was returning from shuttling his two clients twelve miles off the coast of New York City into open water, where a seaplane waited to receive them. As always, he never asked their names or questioned the nature of their business. That information wasn't important to him. What was important was his compensation and how it was provided. The satchel he carried contained one hundred thousand dollars in small bills, just as the transaction had demanded: fifty thousand for each man. Their manner of dress and the expensive jewelry they wore suggested they were probably players in the drug trade. Over the years of offering his services he had come to recognize the signs. Mafia bosses and their capos tended to downplay their appearance and wealth, whereas drug kingpins opted to display their riches. The combined value of the watches and jewelry worn tonight by the two men likely exceeded *Off The Hook's* recent five hundred-thousand-dollar appraisal.

Oleg nodded at the guard. "Not tonight, Earl," he replied. "It's a perfect night. I thought I'd take her out alone, have her all to myself for a change."

Earl laughed. "Can't say that I blame you. If I could afford a boat like yours, you wouldn't see me for days."

Oleg smiled. "You like being on the water?"

The guard nodded. "I grew up in Nantucket. When I was a kid, you couldn't get me off it. I had a small boat. Nothing as fancy as yours, but it served its purpose. I paid my way through college with that boat hosting sunset cruises up and down the coast. Tourists loved it. So did I. My son is as nuts about boats as I am. Says he wants to own a yacht one day. The kid's whip smart. At the rate he's going, he'll probably get it."

"You never thought about growing the business into something bigger?"

"I did," Earl replied. "I opted to go into law enforcement instead. Figured it would be a more stable career choice."

"You were a cop?"

He nodded. "For one day."

"One day? What are you talking about?"

"First day out on my own, I got T-boned by a drunk driver. Totalled my patrol unit and my pelvis at the same time. He died in the crash, so I guess you could say he got the worst of it."

"Jesus! How are you now?"

Earl shrugged. "I have good days and bad days. Today happens to be a good one."

"I'm sorry that happened to you," Oleg said. "I'll bet you would have made a fine officer."

The guard nodded. "Me too." He pointed to the parking lot. "You see those guys over there?"

Oleg glanced across the lot, saw the two men staring at the boats in the marina. "Yes," he replied.

"They were asking about the *Off The Hook*. You know 'em?"

Oleg shook his head. "No, but I've got her listed for sale. Maybe they want to check her out."

The guard checked his watch. "It's 10:30 P.M. Isn't that a little late?" he asked.

Oleg nodded. "Yeah, it is." He paused. "How long have they been here?"

"An hour, maybe longer. You'd think they would have called you first and booked an appointment instead of showing up unannounced."

"That's what I would have done."

"You want me to tell them you're unavailable and send them on their way?"

Oleg shook his head. "Thanks, Earl. It's all right. I've nothing else on my dance card for tonight. If they want to check out the *Hook,* they're welcome to. I'll throw my stuff in my car, then give them the nickel tour."

Earl nodded. "If it's cool with you, it's cool with me."

Oleg winked. "I've got a bottle of Macallan single malt in the galley. If they make me an offer I can't refuse, I'll crack it open. You're welcome to join me for a drink."

Earl smiled. "Sounds good to me. Good luck, Captain."

"Thanks, Earl," Oleg replied. He walked through the security gate and headed for his car.

One of the men saw him, called out. "Mr. Schroeder?"

Oleg opened the trunk, tossed in the satchel, closed the lid. *Mr. Schroeder?* Earl had said nothing to him about the men asking for him by name. The *Off The Hook* was listed on a sales website for used sport fishing boats. All inquiries were conducted through the platform's secure internal messaging system. No personal contact information was made available.

Oleg suddenly felt uneasy.

Something was wrong.

He first thought about the bag of money in the trunk, then the nine-millimetre semi-automatic handgun he kept in the Jaguar's glovebox for protection.

The man called out again. "Sir, could we have a minute of your time?"

Oleg ignored him, double-clicked the fob, unlocked the vehicle, opened the passenger door and glove box, withdrew the weapon, slipped it into his jacket pocket, and closed the door. "If this is about the boat, we'll have to do it another time," he said. "It's been a long day." The second man had disappeared. Oleg glanced around the parking lot, saw no sign of him. In another section of the facility, a vehicle started, revved its engine. Oleg watched it pull out of its parking space and drive in his direction.

Curious and concerned for Oleg's safety the security guard exited his booth and called out. "Everything okay, Captain?"

The stranger answered him. "Everything's fine. Go back to your station."

Earl placed his hand on his sidearm. "I wasn't talking to you, slick."

A black Cadillac Escalade sped around the corner, blocked in Oleg's Jaguar. The driver stepped out of the SUV, drew his weapon.

Earl recognized the gun's silencer too late. The first sound-suppressed round pierced his heart with a quiet *thwup*. The second blew out the back of his head.

The first man removed his gun and pointed it at Oleg as his partner tended to the body of the dead security guard, dragged him inside his booth, closed the door, and then rejoined his partner.

"Hands," the first man said.

Oleg raised his arms as his partner patted him down, relieved him of his weapon and car keys, then opened the Escalade's rear door. "Get in," he ordered.

Oleg climbed into the vehicle. "Who the hell are you?" he asked. "What's this about?"

"You'll know soon enough."

Oleg struggled as a cloth bag was forced over his head, his hands bound. The last thing he felt before darkness enveloped him was the prick of the needle as it pierced his neck. He fell into a deep sleep.

His attacker spoke to his partner. "Call Ferriman. Tell him we've secured the package. I'll follow you in the Jag."

His partner nodded. "Copy that."

6

Safe Passage

MATT AND KYLA waited until the Cigarette boat cleared the lagoon and exited the channel, then walked to the end of the wharf. Matt called out to the man standing in the shadows. "Lorenzo says you're the man to see about a ride."

The man stepped forward. "That is right," he replied. "My name is Xiomara." He extended his hand. "And you are?"

"In need of a lift," Matt replied. He kept his distance, watched the man carefully, sized him up.

Kyla kept her hand cradled around the Glock tucked into her waistband, studied the building behind him for signs of movement, saw none.

Xiomara noted the look of concern on their faces,

retracted his hand. "You can relax, my friends," he said. "There is nothing to fear here in Puerto Lempira. Any dangers you may face will lie in the journey ahead."

"You sound sure of that," Matt said.

Xiomara nodded. "One would be a fool to believe otherwise."

Kyla removed a slip of paper from her pocket, handed it to Xiomara. "Do you know where this is?" she asked.

"I know every square mile of Honduras," Xiomara replied. He unfolded the paper and read the location. "Rus Rus is a three-hour drive. There is only one route from here to there, and it is not safe. You'll be traveling on very rural roads, past Sirsitara and Mocorón. Nicaraguan rebels have been known to cross the border into Rus Rus from Palo Yumpa at night. I strongly recommend you wait until morning to leave. It will be safer to travel then."

"Can you get us there tonight?" Matt asked.

Xiomara nodded. "Yes, if you insist."

"I do."

Xiomara sighed. "Very well. My vehicle is parked behind the building. Come."

Matt spoke as he and Kyla followed the driver. "You drive to Rus Rus often?"

"Many times," Xiomara replied.

"Have you had problems in the past?" Kyla asked.

"I used to. Not anymore"

"The gangs don't give you or your passengers any trouble?"

"My passengers are usually Columbians or Nicaraguans, not Americans."

"That makes a difference?"

"To the gangs and rebels, it does. To them, Americans are a valuable commodity. Besides the drug trade, do you know what earns them the most money?"

"I have a pretty good idea," Matt replied.

"Kidnap for ransom," Xiomara stated. "I've heard that prices start at one million US dollars per person. It can take months of negotiations between the gang leaders and the professionals hired by the families of those they have kidnapped before an amount high enough to secure their release and safe return is agreed upon."

"And if no agreement is reached?" Kyla asked.

"Then the negations end, and the hostages are never seen or heard from again."

"Lovely."

"The biggest mistake one can make down here is under-estimating the gangs," Xiomara stated. "They are much more than thugs. They have foot soldiers whom they use to control the streets, of course. However, their real power and influence lies within their top-tier leadership who run them like Fortune 100 corporations. They are international businesses run by legal and financial professionals. Their annual revenue exceeds that of some countries." Xiomara reached his vehicle, a late-model Volkswagen minibus with tinted windows. He walked to the back of the bus, opened the rear storage compartment. "You can store your bags in here," he said.

"Thanks, but we'll keep them with us," Matt replied.

Xiomara nodded. "As you wish." He slid open the bus's side panel door. The vehicle's cargo space was stacked from floor to ceiling with wooden produce crates, each full of peppers and squash. "You'll be safe back here," he said.

Kyla stared at the dozens of crates. "Where do you expect us to sit?"

Xiomara smiled. "Dear lady, this is why I'm not stopped anymore." He removed the two forward-facing crates and placed them on the ground at his feet, which revealed a hidden door. He opened it.

Matt stepped forward, looked inside, inspected the hollow wooden framework and its makeshift bench seat.

The secret cabin had been constructed to accommodate two passengers seated side by side.

"You'll find you have ample room," Xiomara said. He pointed to the crates on the ground. "Once you're seated inside, I'll close the door and put back these crates, which will hide the compartment. No one will know you're there. The cabin has excellent air circulation, plus I've modified the forward-facing crates so that you can see through them as we drive. If anyone stops us, all they'll see is me taking fresh produce to market."

Matt nodded. "Smart."

Xiomara smiled. "Thank you."

Matt continued. "If you've gone to this degree of effort to secure safe passage for your customers, I'm guessing you also have access to tactical gear and weapons?"

"What do you need?"

"Two vests, plus knives and ammunition. Nine millimetre."

Xiomara pointed to the building's rear entrance. "You'll find everything you need in there. But I suggest you travel light."

Matt nodded. "Show me what you've got."

"How much is this three-hour trip going to cost?" Kyla asked.

"Ten thousand American dollars," Xiomara replied. "Plus the cost of whatever supplies you purchase."

"Done," Matt replied.

Twenty minutes later, seated in the false compartment of the minibus, Matt and Kyla left Puerto Lempira for Rus Rus.

7

Rendition

OLEG AWOKE TO find his hands and feet bound to the arms and legs of a steel office chair. He recognized the two men standing in front of him as his abductors. A third man seated across from him leaned forward, placed his elbows on the wooden table separating them, and spoke.

"Welcome back, Mr. Schroeder," he said. "You've been napping for quite some time. How are you feeling? Can I get you anything? A glass of water, perhaps?"

Oleg took in the starkly appointed room. The walls were comprised of floor-to-ceiling brushed aluminum panels, each patterned with hundreds of small holes. Judging by the unnaturally low volume of the man's voice, Oleg deduced their purpose was to dampen any sound produced within the room. A low-watt light bulb housed within an overhead steel fixture cast the room in more shadow than light. He stared at the man. "Who are you?" he asked.

"Someone in need of information," Ferriman replied.

Oleg stared at his restraints, struggled against them unsuccessfully, then turned his attention back to the stranger. "Your approach to getting it is a little extreme, wouldn't you say?"

"It tends to work."

Oleg glanced at the men standing on either side of his interrogator. "Like I told your bookends, if you want to know more about my boat, make an appointment."

Ferriman leaned back, crossed his arms. "You think you're here because of a boat?"

Oleg smiled. "What can I say? It's one hell of a boat."

"You can't be that stupid."

"I'm not."

"Good. I'll get straight to the point. Who were the passengers on your boat on the night of the explosion?"

"Explosion? What explosion?"

"Don't play games with me, Mr. Schroeder. You know exactly what I'm talking about. The explosion that destroyed the Red Thunder fireworks factory approximately one month ago in New York City."

"Oh, *that* explosion. That was something, wasn't it?"

"Don't try my patience. That's not a good thing."

"Why? You going to beat me up or something?"

"Or something." Ferriman motioned to the agent standing on his left. The man walked behind Oleg, then returned to his position, pushing a small metal cart. He stopped the cart beside the table, stepped back, and awaited further instructions.

Oleg glanced at the three metal syringes lying on the

cart's top tray. "Oh, I get it," he said. "You guys are overdue for your flu shot. Good thinking. It's supposed to be a bad year."

Ferriman stared at Oleg, said nothing, allowed an uncomfortable period of silence to pass between them, then opened a file folder in front of him and began to read.

"Oleg Manfred Schroeder. Age fifty-one. Born in Strasbourg, Germany. The only child of Lina and Adolf Schroeder, both deceased. Educated at the Technical University of Munich. Graduated with dual degrees in engineering and business management. Sponsored into the United States twenty years ago by Monforte, Horvath and Associates, Long Island, New York. Final position Senior Vice-president, Transportation Solutions Division." Ferriman stopped and looked at Oleg. "That's quite a position to have attained within ten years. I'm impressed."

Oleg dismissed the compliment. "What can I tell you? I'm an overachiever."

Ferriman continued. "Wife, Gerta."

Oleg stared coldly at his adversary. "Don't go there."

"Murdered, five years ago. Body found in the trunk of her car. Manner of death: hemorrhage, shock, and asphyxia resulting from aspirated blood. Cause of death: CTI; cut-throat injury resulting in the exposure of the hypopharynx and larynx which was inflicted by a hunting knife discovered by the authorities at the crime scene. No DNA, fingerprints, or trace evidence was recovered. No leads, no suspects, no arrests made to date." Ferriman looked up from the report. "This has been a cold case for five years now."

Oleg said nothing.

Ferriman returned to the document. "Shortly after your wife's untimely demise, you experienced a meltdown at work, took the service elevator to the roof of the building, walked to the edge, then spent the next two hours conversing with an NYPD SWAT negotiator until he managed to talk you down. You were relieved of your position at Monforte-Horvath shortly after that and given a healthy severance package with lifetime medical benefits. Two years later, you purchased the *Off The Hook* and began your sport fishing charter business, which appears to have become quite a successful venture."

"I'm flattered you find my life so interesting," Oleg replied.

"Actually, Mr. Schroeder, what I find most interesting is how a one-man fishing charter has managed to earn six million dollars for its owner in just five years."

Oleg smiled. "What can I say? I'm thrifty. By the way, if you guys are special investigators for the Internal Revenue Service, you need to stop taking your job so seriously. Arm and foot restraints? Really?"

"I think you know that's not who we are."

"Department of the Interior?" Oleg asked. "U.S. Fish and Wildlife Service? I swear, whatever my clients catch is in season. Cross my heart and hope to die. Wait a sec. Scratch that last sentence."

"You're in a Central Intelligence Agency black site, Mr. Schroeder. This is a rendition room. Do you know what that means?"

"That I'll be getting home late and should call someone to feed my hamster?"

"How long you remain here is up to you. Can you guess what happens in this room?"

Oleg stared at the syringes. "I have an idea."

"Well, in the interest of full disclosure, let me tell you.

We ask questions that require answers. These questions pertain to matters of national security. If the detainee, who would be you, is honest and forthright with us, the process goes along without a hitch and is over almost as quickly as it began. We thank you for your cooperation, take you home, and let you get on with your life. But if that detainee, again, you, fails to cooperate with us, or tries to thwart our efforts to seek the truth, we lean on more extreme methods to further that cooperation." Ferriman picked up one of the syringes from the medical cart. "Such as this."

"You're saying that's *not* a flu shot?" Oleg replied.

Ferriman shook his head. "No, Mr. Schroeder. It most assuredly is not." He paused. "So, what's it going to be? The easy way or the hard way?"

"Can I have a minute to think about it?" Oleg asked.

"No, you can't."

Oleg sighed. "Well then, I think I'll go with option number one."

Ferriman returned the syringe to the cart, smiled. "Wise decision."

8

Alive

XIOMARA CALLED OUT as the Volkswagen minibus navigated the narrow two-lane road, his passengers hidden from view inside the secret compartment beneath the wooden crates. "Are you comfortable back there?"

Kyla answered. "Yes, but I'm pretty sure that by the time we reach Rus Rus, I'll have lost my appetite for fresh produce."

Xiomara chuckled. "Better that than not arriving at all."

"Agreed," Kyla replied.

"Can you see through the crates?" Xiomara asked.

"Yes," Matt replied. "Although at this hour, there isn't much to see."

"There is no moon tonight," Xiomara replied. "On these roads, that can be a cause for concern."

"Why is that?"

"Gangs and guerrillas prefer to attack on nights like this," Xiomara explained. "They take advantage of the absence of moonlight and use it to their advantage. Keep your weapons handy, but do not engage with them unless it becomes necessary. There are only three of us, and I never carry a weapon."

"If this route is so dangerous, why not arm yourself?" Matt asked.

"For the sake of appearances," Xiomara replied. "What threat is a lowly, unarmed vegetable vendor to them? And when I ask if they're hungry and offer them a crate or two of fresh produce, they accept it and let me continue on my way. It is a small tax to pay to be left unharmed."

"You've got this figured out," Matt said.

"I understand people. And I am a good negotiator."

"I'll say," Kyla replied. "You negotiated ten grand out of my partner with no objection. I'm impressed."

Matt smiled and shook his head.

Xiomara laughed. "Are you suggesting I should have asked for more? Twenty-thousand dollars, perhaps?"

"He'd probably have paid it," Kyla replied.

Xiomara glanced in his rearview mirror. Through the slit in the crate, Matt could see him smiling. "Perhaps your beautiful friend should negotiate for you from now on," he said. "She'll save you a fortune in the long run."

"Perhaps she should," Matt replied.

Xiomara slowed the van abruptly.

"What's wrong?" Matt asked.

"I'm not sure," Xiomara replied. "I've never seen this before."

Matt and Kyla stared out through the crates. In the distance, an orange glow illuminated the treetops.

"You smell that?" Kyla asked.

Matt nodded. "Smoke."

Xiomara approached the blind turn in the road ahead with caution. "This doesn't feel right," he said.

"Is there another route we can take to get to Rus Rus from here?" Kyla asked.

Xiomara shook his head. "No."

"What do you think it could be?" Matt asked.

"A car fire, perhaps," Xiomara replied.

"Can you drive around it?"

"Not if it's what I think it is."

"Meaning?"

"Sometimes the gangs will set fire to a car and block the road, forcing motorists to stop."

"Why?"

"To rob them, or worse."

"You really need to rethink the whole refuse-to-carry-a-gun thing, Xiomara," Matt said.

Xiomara sighed. "You might be right about that."

Matt and Kyla removed their weapons. "If they order you out of the vehicle," Matt said, "slide the side door open as quickly as you can, then remove the crates and offer them your produce. If the situation escalates, I want to be able to get out of here and have a clear line of sight when I fire. If there's gunplay, drop to the ground and get under the bus. You should be safe there until it's over. Got it?"

Xiomara answered nervously. "Okay."

"All right. Move ahead, slowly."

Xiomara eased the minibus ahead and rounded the corner. "Oh my god!" he exclaimed.

An older woman stood on the shoulder of the road, staring down a laneway at her burning home, watching as the flames that threatened to consume her modest abode rose higher and higher into the air. She stepped onto the road and waved her arms frantically.

Xiomara stopped the minibus.

Kyla turned to Matt. "We can't drive on," she said. "We have to help her!"

"There's no cellular service out here," Xiomara said as he opened his door and exited the bus. "It's a dead zone." He lifted the lever, slid back the sliding door on Matt's side of the bus, quickly removed the crates, set them down, then opened the secret door. Matt hurried out of the compartment with Kyla right behind him.

Xiomara tried to calm the woman as he spoke. "Hay alguien más en la casa?" he asked.

The woman cried and pleaded. "Si. Mi marido y mi nieto. Ayudame! Ayudame!"

Xiomara turned to Matt and Kyla. "She says her husband and grandson are still in the house. She's asking for our help."

Matt answered by racing down the laneway toward the house.

Kyla turned to Xiomara. "Stay with her," she ordered, then chased after Matt.

As Matt reached the front of the small house, the heat of the white-hot fire instantly pushed him back. Above him, the second-floor windows hissed, then blew out of their frames from the immense heat that had built up behind them. The rooms above were now fully involved. Wisps of smoke seeped from between the wooden shingles, followed by flickers of orange flame.

Matt called out. "Can anybody hear me?"

A faint response came from a weak knock behind the front door.

"They're at the door," Matt said to Kyla. "Look around. Find something we can use to break it down."

Matt and Kyla scoured the property, searched for an implement that would be capable of helping them gain entrance to the burning house.

"Over here!" Kyla yelled.

Matt ran to her, picked up a metal milk collection container. In the barn behind the small property, a cow cried out in fear, having sensed the presence of the fire and the threat it imposed. "It'll have to do. Come on!"

"We're only going to get one shot at this," Matt said. "I'll break down the door, then we'll enter the house. If we can't locate the man and his grandson immediately, we're out of there. The second floor doesn't have much more life left. When it falls, it'll come down right on top of us. You ready?"

"Ready."

"On me in three, two, *one*!"

Matt swung the milking can with all his might. The heavy container failed to break down the wooden door but split the frame. Matt stood with his back to the door, then kicked it violently.

The door flew open.

On the floor in front of them, an old man lay atop a young boy, shielding him from the flames as they crept toward them with deadly intent.

"I've got the old man," Matt yelled. "You grab the boy."

Matt pulled the semi-conscious man to his feet, dropped low, shifted his weight, hoisted him onto his shoulder.

Kyla picked up the boy in her arms and headed outside.

The child coughed as he breathed in the cool night air. Kyla set him down on the ground. His grandmother ran to him and took him in her arms.

Xiomara ran to Matt and helped him carry the old man a safe distance from the burning house. Matt laid the man on his back, put his ear to his mouth, listened. A faint breath of air brushed his face. "He's alive," Matt said. He pointed to a bucket across the yard in front of the barn. "Check it for water."

Xiomara ran to the bucket, picked it up, ran back. "Only a little," he said.

"A little is all we'll need," Matt replied. He dipped his hand in the cold water and splashed it on the old man's face.

The man slowly came around. He coughed, then struggled to sit up. "Mi nieto!" he said.

Matt wiped away the water, pointed to the boy.

The grandfather crawled across the ground, joined his precious family, fell into their arms.

Together, they watched the fire claim what remained of their home.

Matt rose to his feet.

Kyla walked to him. "You okay?" she asked.

Matt nodded. "Yeah."

Xiomara joined them, pointed. "Look," he said. "The road."

The three watched as a group of men jumped from the rear of a flatbed truck that had pulled in behind the minibus.

"We need to leave," Xiomara said. "Now."

"Who are they?" Matt asked.

"Members of Mara Salvatrucha, the deadliest gang in all

of Honduras." Xiomara spied a break in the tree line at the back of the property. "Quick," he said. "Follow me!"

Kyla looked at the small family huddled together on the cold ground. "What about them?" she asked.

"Don't worry," Xiomara replied. "The gang will not leave them like this. They'll help them, but eventually they'll ask for something in return. But if they find you here, that will be a different story. We must get out of here before they see us. *Hurry!*"

He ran toward the trees.

Matt and Kyla followed.

9

So Many Bundles

FERRIMAN MOTIONED TO the agent standing to his left. The man leaned forward, listened as Ferriman whispered in his ear, nodded, then left the room. He returned a few seconds later, laptop in hand, placed the computer on the table in front of the director, and returned to his post.

Oleg observed the military manner in which the agent carried out the request, then stood sentry still behind his boss. "Wow," he said. "He's well trained. Is he housebroken?"

The agent glared at Oleg.

Ferriman said nothing. He raised the laptop cover, waited for the device to power up, then turned the machine around, showed Oleg the screen.

The center of the black screen was occupied by the

Central Intelligence Agency's red, white, blue, and yellow logo.

"So you really are CIA," Oleg replied.

"How observant," Ferriman replied. He tapped the touchpad, took the device out of sleep mode, opened a folder on the desktop containing a single video file. "Tell me if this looks familiar to you," he said, then pressed the PLAY icon.

Oleg watched the video and listened to the accompanying news report.

"Well?" Ferriman asked.

Oleg shrugged. "Sure, I've seen it. The fireworks factory explosion. All of New York has seen this footage. So what?"

"Anything look familiar to you?"

"Should it?"

"I would think so."

"Can't say that it does."

"You don't recognize your own boat, Mr. Schroeder?"

Oleg stared at the screen as Ferriman played the news report once again, pausing it at the exact second the name *Off The Hook* became visible on the fishing boat's transom. The look of shock on Oleg's face spoke for him.

"I'm going to give you one last chance to come clean with me," Ferriman said. "If you still refuse to cooperate, I won't waste any more time with you. We'll go straight to option two. Trust me, Mr. Schroeder, you won't like that."

Oleg looked down, stared at his bindings.

"The man and woman standing at the back of the boat," Ferriman asked. "Who are they? What are their names?"

Oleg shook his head, lied. "I don't know who they are."

"You don't know the names of the people who pay you so generously for your services?"

"No."

Ferriman nodded. "I see." He turned to the agent on his right. "Bring in the bag. And a lighter."

"Yes, sir," the agent replied. He left the room.

"Bag?" Oleg asked. "What's that? Some interrogation thing?"

Ferriman smiled. "In your case, I'd call it more of an incentive to hasten your cooperation."

The agent returned with Oleg's leather satchel, set it on the table, placed a cigarette lighter beside it, and stepped back.

"Hey," Oleg said. "That's mine!"

"Yes, it is," Ferriman replied. "My men are thorough, Mr. Schroeder. They retrieved it from the trunk of your car before bringing you here, along with the loaded gun you had in your jacket pocket."

"You mean before they kidnapped me?"

Ferriman shrugged. "Semantics. You're here now. That's what's important." He pushed his chair back as he stood. Its feet squeaked as they dragged across the worn linoleum floor. He unzipped the satchel, looked inside, examined the contents, and smiled at Oleg. "There's quite a lot of money in here," he said. He removed one of the bundles of cash. "So many bundles, all in small denominations and secured with elastic bands. This has all the earmarks of a cartel payment. I'll bet if I were to send these bills out to our lab for analysis, they would likely test positive for cocaine residue. Am I right?"

Oleg stared at the stack of bills Ferriman held in his hand. "I wouldn't know anything about that," he said.

"No?"

"No."

Ferriman nodded. "I see. Well, at the very least, I'm sure we can both agree that these funds were obtained illegally."

Oleg protested. "Last I heard, it's still legal for my clients to pay me in cash."

"You must cater to a very exclusive sport fishing clientele for them to pay you so much money, Mr. Schroeder. And if that's the case, I'm sure you'll be able to replace it very easily."

"What do you mean, replace it?"

Ferriman retrieved the butane lighter from the table, flipped back its silver lid, thumbed the flint wheel. The spark found the moist wick, set it ablaze. He touched the flame to the corner of the stack of bills, then turned it over in his hand and watched it burn.

Oleg fought against his restraints. He tried to pull himself to his feet, then fell back in his chair. "Are you insane?" he yelled. "That's a grand you just lit up!"

Ferriman glanced at the agent standing to his left and then at Oleg. "Perhaps I should send out Agent Washburn to pick up a bag of marshmallows? We could have ourselves a little bonfire."

"Fuck you!"

Ferriman stared at Oleg. "Does that work for you, Agent Washburn?" he asked.

Washburn nodded. "Works great for me, sir."

"Then a bonfire it is." Ferriman pulled a second stack of bills out of the bag, set it afire.

"You son of a bitch!" Oleg yelled as he watched his money burn. "That belongs to me! I earned it!"

Ferriman tossed the burning bills onto the table, retrieved a third stack from the satchel. "You want me to keep going, Mr. Schroeder? I can do this over and over until all the money is gone. Is that what you want?"

Oleg watched the paper begin to smoke, curl, and finally disintegrate. Tendrils of ash floated up into the air.

"How much is that so far?" the CIA director asked. "Two thousand dollars? You have ninety-eight thousand left. Do you want to keep it, or shall I continue?"

Defeated, Oleg stared at the burning money. "I want to keep it."

Ferriman set down the lighter, closed the satchel, slid it across the table to Oleg. "Then it's yours. But only if you tell me what I want to know. Who are the people standing at the back of your boat watching the building burn?"

"I don't know his name," Oleg said. "Just hers."

"And that would be?"

Oleg looked up, met the director's eyes. "Her name is Kyla Reese."

10

Hostiles

MATT, KYLA, AND XIOMARA crept through the thick enclave of trees behind the old barn until they reached the side of the road. They dropped low, observed the gang members as they examined Xiomara's minibus. One of the men called out, then waved to his associate to join him at the vehicle.

"What did he say?" Matt asked.

"He told him to come to him," Xiomara replied, "that there's something he needed to see."

"He found the secret compartment."

Xiomara nodded. "So it appears."

"What do we do now?" Kyla asked. "All our gear is in there."

"We don't have a choice," Matt said. "We'll have to engage."

Kyla nodded. "You have a count?"

"Eight," Matt replied. "Two at the minibus, two at the flatbed, plus four headed down the laneway towards the family."

"Think we can go less lethal? Take them out by hand?"

Matt shook his head. "No way. They're heavily armed. AK-47 assault rifles. This has to be done fast. Headshots, if possible, then we'll take their weapons."

Kyla nodded. "Copy that."

Matt turned to Xiomara. "Once Kyla is in position, we'll move together. Stay behind me."

Xiomara answered nervously. "I'm a produce vendor, not a fighter."

"Tonight, you're both," Matt replied. He turned to Kyla. "When you're ready, whistle once. We'll move simultaneously."

"Got it."

"Go."

Matt watched Kyla navigate her way back through the trees. When he had lost sight of her, he removed his weapon, chambered a round.

To Xiomara, he said, "This is going to go down fast, so stay glued to me. If I get hit and fall, you pick up my gun and fire. Keep firing until you're out of bullets or they're all dead. Hesitate and you're a dead man. You have a family?"

Xiomara nodded.

"You want to see them again?"

"Yes."

"Then don't screw this up."

Matt stepped closer to the side of the road, short of breaking cover from the tree line. "Get ready," he said.

Out of the darkness came a short whistle, followed by gunfire, then panicked screams.

Matt broke from the cover of the tree line with Xiomara at his back and advanced quickly up the road, his attention front sight focused on the human targets ahead.

Four gunshots rang out from Kyla's position with no retaliatory fire.

A second whistle.

Four hostiles down.

The two men rummaging through the minibus heard the shots and stepped into the road.

Matt dropped them quickly, then turned his attention to the remaining gang members as they ran back to their truck to escape the sudden ambush. His first round struck the driver in his back, took him down. Matt watched the second man raise his weapon, point it in his direction, then heard a shot.

The round had not come from the man's rifle.

Kyla's bullet had found its mark.

Matt watched him drop to the ground.

Kyla stepped into view. "You okay?" she asked.

Matt nodded. "Nice shot."

"It looked like you could use a little help."

"I had it under control."

Kyla smiled. "Sure you did."

Matt looked toward the burning house. The second floor had surrendered to the fire and fallen, reducing the structure to a mass of flickering flames. Glowing embers lifted into the air, threatened the nearby trees.

"How's the family doing?" he asked.

"Well, let's see," Kyla replied. "Their house just burned to the ground; they nearly died in the fire, and now they have eight dead bodies on their property. If I were to guess, I'd say not too well."

"At least they're alive."

Kyla nodded. "Can't argue with that."

"We need to hide the bodies and the truck," Xiomara said. "The Mara Salvatrucha are like wild dogs. They run up and down these roads at night in packs, protecting their territory. Another group will pass through here soon. If they find their men dead on the road, they'll question the family, probably torture them, whether they can tell them what happened or not. From what I've heard about their methods, they'd have been better off dying in the fire."

Matt nodded. "All right. Talk to them. Kyla and I will collect their weapons and cell phones and move the bodies out of the way. I'll drive the truck into the barn, get it out of sight."

"Understood," Xiomara said, then hurried down the driveway to speak with the family.

Matt approached the dead men lying on the ground beside the minibus, picked up their assault rifles, carried them to the vehicle, and tossed them into the footwell of the secret compartment. "We should have kept driving," he said.

Kyla nodded. "I know. But we didn't have a choice."

"Someone will have heard the gunshots. They'll be curious. What if they show up?"

"At this time of night? I don't think so. They'll attribute it to the gangs popping off rounds."

Matt walked to the flatbed, picked up a third assault rifle, and then relieved the man he had fatally shot of the Glock pistol tucked into his waistband. He took their weapons and phones to the minibus. "I hope you're right," he said.

"Me too."

Matt returned to the flatbed, found the keys in the ignition, hopped into the cab, and started the engine. "Check on Xiomara and the family," he said. "Make sure they're all right. I'll hide this in the barn. After that, we're out of here."

Kyla nodded. "Copy that."

11

One Last Piece Of Advice

"TELL ME MORE about Kyla Reese," Ferriman asked. "Who is she to you, and how did you come to know her?"

"She's an acquaintance," Oleg replied. "I don't know her well at all. She helped me out of a jam a long time ago. I gave her my number and told her that if she ever needed a favor, I would help her if I could. I never thought I'd hear from her again."

"But you did."

Oleg nodded. "Yes."

"What did she want?"

"Safe passage out to international waters for her and a friend."

"And you were able to provide her with that?"

"To a point."

"What do you mean?"

"My vessel has a limited nautical range, so I called in a marker. I know someone who races Cigarette boats and exports cargo that may or may not be illegal from Cuba to Florida. He owes me money. I called him and asked if he could get them out of the country sight unseen. He said it wouldn't be a problem and would make it happen. I told him I'd consider his debt paid in full if he did this for me. He told me not to worry. So that's what he did. I shuttled Kyla and her friend to his boat, and we said goodbye. That was the last I've seen of them."

"And you trusted him to do this?"

Oleg nodded. "We run in the same circles. He knows better than to try anything stupid with me, let alone any of my friends."

"What is his name?"

"Do we really have to bring him into this?"

Ferriman stood, removed a wad of bills from Oleg's leather satchel, picked up the lighter, and lit the flame. "Yes, we do," he replied.

Oleg cried out. "For God's sake, stop burning up my cash! All right, all right. His name is Ashton Tucker."

"And the name of his speed boat?"

"Cerberus."

"Where can we find Mr. Tucker?"

"Damned if I know. Anywhere and everywhere. He's always on the water. He's a twenty-something trust fund kid who likes fast boats, fast cars, and fast women. And not necessarily in that order."

"We need to speak with him."

"Yeah? Well, good luck with that. He's pretty much impossible to reach."

"But you have his number."

"Yes."

"So you can reach him."

"Yes."

"Then that's what you're going to do."

"How about I give you his contact information and you reach out to him directly? There's no reason for me to get involved."

"You're already involved, Mr. Schroeder. *Very* involved."

Oleg shook his head. "Dammit."

"Take out your phone and make the call," Ferriman said. "Tell Mr. Tucker you need him to arrange another pick up like he did for Kyla Reese."

"His services don't come cheap. I forgave a fifty grand gambling debt for him to make that happen for me. He'll want to be paid."

"Tell him the situation is urgent and that the client is willing to pay any amount he asks, in cash, with one caveat. He needs to be out of the country by noon tomorrow. Instruct him to rendezvous with you where he did last time. My men will accompany you."

"You're just going to talk to him, right? No black ops interrogation stuff, right?"

"All we're looking for are answers to a few important questions, Mr. Schroeder."

"What about me?"

Ferriman shrugged. "What about you?"

"What happens now?"

"I don't understand."

"Are you going to let me go?"

"Of course. That's what I said, didn't I?"

"Forgive me if I thought you were lying... you know, being the CIA and all."

"All I'm after is information, Mr. Schroeder. Which you have been good enough to provide. Now, as promised, my men will drive you back to your car. But first, please make that call. And put it on speaker."

"Yeah, sure," Oleg said.

Ferriman instructed his men to free Oleg's hands, then listened as he called Ashton Tucker, explained his fake client's dire situation, made the request, and agreed to pay him fifty thousand dollars for an afternoon's work. Oleg terminated the call. "That's it," he said. "10 A.M. tomorrow. Have your men meet me at my slip at nine. We'll leave immediately."

Agent Washburn leaned forward, whispered into the director's ear, informed him of their requirement to shoot and kill the security guard at the time of Oleg's abduction, which Oleg had not seen. Ferriman nodded. He turned to Oleg. "It seems there was a bit of a problem at the marina when my men picked you up."

"A problem?"

"Nothing you need to be concerned about. However, there is a strong possibility the marina parking lot will be closed tomorrow. Is there a way for you to avoid the lot and access your boat from the water?"

Oleg nodded. "I can park in the water taxi lot. They'll shuttle me straight to the slip."

"Good," Ferriman replied. "Do that. Minimize your contact with others. Drive your boat to the public pier adjacent to the former site of Red Thunder Fireworks. My men will be waiting for you at 9 A.M."

"You're ordering me around like I work for you."

"That's because, until tomorrow, when our business is concluded and your cooperation is no longer necessary, you do."

Oleg said nothing.

Ferriman pointed to the door. "You're free to go, Mr. Schroeder. My men will return you to your vehicle."

Oleg stared at the satchel on the table.

"Yes," Ferriman said. "You can take the money. After all, it belongs to you. You earned it, remember?"

Oleg picked up the bag. "Right," he replied, then walked to the door.

"Before you leave," Ferriman said, "let me remind you of one thing."

Oleg turned. "What's that?"

"You were never here. Our conversation never took place."

Oleg paused. "What conversation?"

Ferriman nodded. "Exactly."

Agent Washburn approached Oleg, a black cloth hood in his hand.

"That again?" Oleg asked.

"This location is confidential. We plan to keep it that way." He handed Oleg the hood. "Put it on. We'll remove it when we get to your car." He held out his hand. "Hand me the bag."

Oleg paused, then handed the agent the leather satchel containing his ninety-eight thousand dollars. He slipped the hood over his head.

Washburn opened the door, took him by his arm, led him out of the room.

"I'll be counting that money when I get to my car," Oleg said.

"I'm sure you will," Washburn replied.

"It all better be there."

Washburn dug his thumb into the back of Oleg's arm as he escorted him down the hallway.

"Shut up and walk," he said.

12

Dos Ángeles

THE OLD MAN stood in stunned silence, cradling his wounded arm, and watching as the remains of his fire-leveled home crackled and popped as Matt backed the gang's truck past him down the. Wisps of smoke rose from the ashes. A gentle breeze passed through the jumble of smoldering timbers, resuscitated the fire, and breathed life back into it. Here and there, flames reached up from the pyre, struggled to survive, then died, but not before casting the property in an eerie orange light.

Matt parked the truck in the barn and exited the structure. He closed the door behind him and walked to Kyla. The couple's grandson clung to her, his head buried in her side, afraid to look at the place where only moments ago their house had stood. Kyla tried her best to console him but to no avail.

Xiomara stood with the man's wife, assisting her as she did what little she could to tend to her husband's wound.

"How is he?" Matt asked.

Xiomara shook his head. "Not good. He needs to see a doctor. Better yet, be taken to a hospital."

"Let me see."

The man moaned as Matt pulled back the makeshift sling into which his wife had placed his arm. He pulled a cell phone from his pocket, which he had taken from a dead gang member, powered it up, and inspected the burn in the phone's dim light. The man's entire right forearm was red. The skin appeared dry and absent of blisters.

"How bad is it?" Xiomara asked.

"He's lucky," Matt replied. "Only the epidermis, the outer layer of his skin, was burned. If he's lucky, scarring will be minimal." Matt scanned the property and saw what he was looking for. He handed Xiomara the phone. "Wait here," he said.

"Where are you going?" Xiomara asked. "I don't know how to treat this!"

"I do," Matt said. He turned to Kyla. "We need to talk."

Kyla nodded and glanced at the boy's grandmother. She walked over, took her grandson's hand, and led him to his grandfather.

Kyla followed Matt as he walked toward the barn. "How's the grandfather?" she asked.

"He'll be fine. It's us I'm concerned about."

"Meaning?"

Matt knelt, broke off a long leaf from an aloe vera plant, stood. "We can't stay here another minute. This will keep the burn from getting infected long enough for him to get to a hospital where somebody can properly treat it. They have a car. It's in the barn. His wife will have to drive him. We can't. I'm concerned about the fire. It makes sense that no one would respond to the gunshots. The National Police are probably a rare sight on this road. But the fire department is another story. If someone saw the flames or smelled the smoke, they might have called it in. If that's the case, they could be here any minute. We need to move fast."

"What do you want me to do?" Kyla asked.

"Help me drag the bodies behind the barn."

"Copy that."

"I know what you're thinking, Kyla," Matt said. "You want to do more to help these people. So do I. But the bottom line is, we can't."

Kyla nodded. "I know."

"All right," Matt said. "Let's get this over with."

Matt and Kyla rejoined Xiomara and the ailing family. He bit into the aloe vera leaf, pulled back the tough skin, and exposed its gelatinous core. The inside of the leaf revealed a thick, gooey gel.

He instructed Xiomara. "Apply the gel to his arm, fingers, and hand. Who knows how long it'll be before a doctor sees him, so spread it on thick. Kyla and I will dispose of the bodies."

Xiomara nodded. "Okay."

The grandmother smiled, spoke to Xiomara, pointed to Matt and Kyla.

"What did she say?" Matt asked.

"She asked who the two of you are. She called you her *dos ángeles*. Her two angels."

"I'm the farthest thing from an angel she's ever going to meet," Matt replied. "But thank her just the same."

"Same goes for me," Kyla said. "Tell her we're happy her family is safe and that no one was seriously hurt."

Xiomara nodded. "I will."

"You'll have to apologize to them for what we have to do next," Matt said. "We need to dump the bodies behind their barn."

Xiomara translated the message.

The old man replied in Spanish, then spat on the ground.

"What did he say?" Matt asked.

"He said they're devils anyway... that you should throw them onto the embers, set them on fire, and send them back to whatever hell they came from."

Matt smiled. "I'm sure they're already on their way."

Xiomara nodded, then returned to treating the man's badly burned arm.

One by one, Matt and Kyla dragged the corpses of the dead gang members to the rear of the property and piled them in a heap behind the barn.

As they walked up the driveway, Matt suddenly stopped.

"What is it," Kyla asked.

"You hear that? In the distance?"

Kyla listened, nodded. "Sirens."

"Come on," Matt said.

Together they ran up the driveway to Xiomara.

"We have to leave right now," Matt said. "The authorities are coming. I don't know if it's police or fire, but we're not waiting around to find out."

"I haven't finished treating his arm," Xiomara objected.

"His wife knows what to do. Now let's go."

Xiomara issued last-minute instructions to the man's

wife, then ran after Matt and Kyla to the minibus as the wailing siren drew closer.

Matt and Kyla slipped into the secret compartment as emergency lights flashed off the treetops on the roadway behind them.

Matt yelled from inside the compartment. "Go! Go! Go!"

Xiomara started the minibus and hit the gas.

The vehicle lurched ahead, accelerated, reached the turn, rounded the corner. Xiomara spied a dirt road, pulled in, braked to a hard stop, then killed the engine and turned off the headlights.

The three waited and listened.

Xiomara checked his rearview mirror, cracked his window.

The siren had stopped.

"Fire department," he said. "Someone must have reported the blaze. They're at the property. We're safe now."

"Not if they find the bodies," Matt said. "Which they probably will. The old folks will have no choice but to tell them how they ended up at the back of their barn."

Xiomara started the minibus, backed out of the dirt lane onto the main road, hit the gas. "That was close," he said.

"Too close," Matt said. "Do me a favor, Xiomara."

"Of course," Xiomara replied. "Name it."

"If you see any more fires on the way to Rus Rus, don't stop."

Xiomara nodded. "Yes, sir."

13

Hell Of A Thing

THE WATER TAXI approached the marina, slowed, putted to a stop. Oleg thanked the shuttle pilot and tipped him, then climbed the access ladder and stood at the end of the wharf. He observed the parking lot ten slips ahead. Ribbons of black and red police tape circled the security guard's booth and extended across the lot, restricting vehicular and pedestrian traffic from entering the area. A street cop posted at the entrance to the lot was busy turning away cars, preventing them from entering the crime scene, while plainclothes detectives walked the lot, made notes, and conversed with one another.

"Hell of a thing, isn't it?"

Oleg looked in the direction of the voice. In the slip across from the *Off The Hook*, a man stood sipping his morning coffee and watching the police officers as they conducted their investigation. Oleg knew him: John Simmons, former yacht club commodore and all-around busybody. There was nothing Simmons didn't know about the goings on at the club. Not because the information was openly shared with him, but because he made it his business to find out.

"Cops made me park my brand new wheels two blocks over and take the damn water taxi here," Simmons stated. "Bought it two days ago. Porsche 911 GT3 RS. Racing yellow. Cost me three hundred grand. Gorgeous. Instead of parking it here where I can keep my eye on it, it's sitting on the street, eye candy for any degenerate car thief who wants to try to steal it."

Oleg waited for Simmons to stop talking. If two personality traits could never be attributed to him, they were brevity and humility.

"What do you mean," he asked, "hell of a thing?"

"What happened to Earl."

"Jesus Christ, John. Just answer the question."

Offended by the sharp remark, Simmons stared at Oleg, then responded. "Someone shot him dead. Happened late last night from what I heard. I tried to pull more information out of the cops, but they're not talking, not even to me. I told them I was the club's former commodore, but they didn't seem to care. Wouldn't you think that title would pull a little weight with them? Figures, I guess. Even if those yahoo's combined their salaries, they still couldn't come up with enough dough to cover our annual membership dues. I guess that's why we get to sit on our boats drinking coffee all morning while they mop up the mess. Am I right?"

Oleg ignored the offensive comment. "Did they catch who did it?"

Simmons shrugged. "They wouldn't say."

"Did you ask?"

Simmons took a final swig of his coffee, stared at Oleg. "What do you think, Schroeder? Of course, I asked. I'm not as dumb as you look. It's an active investigation, so no, they wouldn't say. Must have been bloody though."

"What makes you say that?"

"The crime scene tape. It's red and black, not yellow and black."

"So?"

"My ex-brother-in-law's a cop. He told me the difference. They only use red and black tape if there's blood at the scene. They consider it a biohazard. You know, blood diseases and all that crap."

Oleg checked his watch: 8:15 A.M. He would need every one of the next forty-five minutes if he was to meet the agents at the public dock beside Red Thunder Fireworks on time for nine o'clock.

Simmons called out as Oleg unlocked his cabin door. "Any takers yet?"

"Takers?"

"To buy your boat."

Oleg shook his head. "Too soon. The ad only went live a few days ago."

"What about the guys who spoke to you the other night?"

Oleg felt a chill run down his spine. He opened the door, climbed the ladder to the bridge, started the engine, climbed back down, removed the mooring lines, tossed them onto the deck, and glanced nonchalantly at Simmons. "Guys? What guys?"

"Ann Farnsworthy said she saw a couple of guys talking to you as she pulled out of the parking lot."

Oleg shook his head. "She's mistaken. It wasn't me."

"You weren't here two nights ago?"

"What are you, Simmons, a cop? I just told you I wasn't here."

Simmons raised his hands in surrender. "Fine, you weren't here. Geez, someone's touchy this morning."

"I have things on my mind, and a busy day ahead is all."

"Well, you better be prepared to make yourself available later."

"Why do you say that?"

"Because Ann left here less than an hour ago. She parked on the street behind me. We talked on the way over in the water taxi. Said she'd left her laptop on her boat and needed to stop by to pick it up. The cops talked to both of us. I didn't have anything useful to tell them, but they seemed pretty interested when Ann mentioned seeing you. She's a corporate CEO and damn smart. How do you suppose she got that wrong?"

"Beats me," Oleg replied. "Could be she saw the guy on the boat next to mine. We look a little alike. He and his wife are traveling. They've rented the slip for the month."

Simmons crossed his arms and stared at Oleg, as though deciding whether to believe him. Finally, he spoke. "Renters, huh?"

"Yeah."

"How come I didn't know about this?"

Oleg sighed. "I don't know, John. Maybe because it's none of your business?"

"You've got quite an attitude, Schroeder. You know that?"

"So I've been told."

"Where are you headed?"

"Out."

"I don't suppose you could be more specific. You know... in case the cops come around asking for you."

"If the cops want to waste their time talking to me, I'll gladly talk to them. They'll just have to do it over the boat's radio. I don't have time to be interviewed right now."

Simmons smiled. "I'll be sure to tell them that."

Oleg climbed up to the bridge, backed the *Off The Hook* out of her slip, and called out as he pulled away from the wharf. "You do that, Simmons."

14

No Such Luck

MATT SPOKE TO Kyla as they passed through Sirsitara. "Of all the places to choose to go in Honduras, why Rus Rus?"

"I spent time there years ago," Kyla replied. "It's a tiny hamlet just five miles from the Nicaraguan border. It's pretty much all forest. There's a grass airstrip and a community hospital, if that's what you want to call it, and that's about it. Only fifty or so families live there. It's as off the radar as it gets. Mabitah, which is the closest village, is a fifty-minute walk. But like most of Honduras, it's dangerous. There's no law enforcement presence. If there's a problem, the villagers handle it themselves, and swiftly. While there, I heard a commotion outside my hut one afternoon, then watched an elder drag a teenager into the middle of the village. He'd been caught stealing. The elder held him down, drew a machete, then cut off his hand. His parents put up no resistance whatsoever. They just walked the boy to the hospital to have the amputation treated. I later learned it was the first criminal act to occur in the village in ten years. I'll bet it's also been the last."

"What brought you there?"

"I was part of an eight-member team tasked with gathering intel in the region. The Honduran government had asked the agency for help. Locals had reported a significant increase in air traffic into and out of the Rus Rus airstrip. The Honduran's didn't know that we'd already picked up chatter and had our eye on it for some time. We suspected Nicaraguans and Guatemalans were using it as a transfer point for cocaine, cash, weapons shipments, and human trafficking. Before that, the airstrip had only been used by NGO's, outreach ministries, and relief organizations. Being surrounded by mountains and jungle provided the perfect cover for clandestine activities."

"What happened?"

"We shut it down. Hard. We caught wind of a meet that was to go down between Abelardo Lopez and Miguel Bautista."

Matt nodded. "I've heard of them. They're Nicaraguan and Guatemalan warlords."

"That's right."

"What happened?"

"We kept eyes on the airstrip for a week. At one o'clock in the morning, Overwatch reported a small plane approaching the airstrip. It touched down and was followed fifteen minutes later by another. We took up tactical positions in the surrounding forest and watched Lopez disembark from one aircraft and Bautista from the other with an entourage of their top lieutenants. There was a small supply building at the end of the airstrip. That's where they gathered to hold their meeting. When the last man entered and closed the door, we moved in. Our sniper took out the poor bastard who'd been ordered to remain outside and guard the door. We extracted his body and waited. Forty-five minutes later, they stepped outside. We identified ourselves, and they responded as we figured they would. The firefight was a joke. It lasted about ten seconds. They had no cover and no means of escape. We took out everyone but Lopez and Bautista. We knew it would be a political feather in America's cap if the president of Honduras got to take credit for the takedown, so we packed them on a plane, flew them directly to Tegucigalpa, and handed them over to the Federal Police. We returned to Rus Rus, packed our gear, and shipped out the next day. I never forgot the place. It might be dangerous, but the people are beautiful. They're just like everyone else on the planet. They want to live a peaceful life and be content with what they have. It's not their fault that their country has been overrun by gangs and their political leadership is corrupt."

Xiomara had been listening to the conversation. "I remember watching the newscast of the arrests of Lopez and Bautista," he said. "That was you?"

"Yes," Kyla replied. "Me and my team."

"So, both of you are CIA?"

"Used to be," Matt said. "Not anymore."

"If you're no longer active, why the need for weapons?"

"We shouldn't be having this discussion, Xiomara," Matt said. "It's not safe for you to know this information."

"Need I remind you that you're sitting in a secret compartment in my minibus?" Xiomara replied. "Trust me, you're not the first to sit back there. I've overhead more than my fair share of conversations, which I probably shouldn't have. I make it a point to remind my customers that my silence is included in the price of my service. I've never broken that trust, and I don't intend to start now."

"I believe you, Xiomara," Kyla said. "Thank you."

Xiomara smiled. "You're welcome."

"How much longer until we reach Rus Rus?" Matt asked.

"Two hours," Xiomara replied. "Assuming we don't run into any more trouble."

"You mean from the gangs?"

Xiomara nodded. "The Mara Salvatrucha keeps a close watch on their people. Those men you killed will be missed. Someone will come looking for them very soon. When they find out they've been murdered, they'll scour the region in search of their killers. It's imperative that you remain out of sight. If anyone questioned by the gang admits to seeing two lone Americans in this part of the country at this hour, they won't hesitate to point the finger of blame at you. It's been their experience that the only Americans ever seen around here are government agents. Quite frankly, I don't think you realize how much danger you are actually in just by being here."

Matt turned to Kyla. "I don't suppose your friend could have booked us on a nicely appointed cruise ship instead of a cargo ship, huh?"

Kyla smiled and shook her head. "No such luck."

15

42 Tiger

OLEG DOCKED AT the public wharf just down from the former site of Red Thunder fireworks company at precisely 9:00 A.M. Agent Washburn and his partner, Hobbs, stood waiting for him to arrive.

Washburn checked his watch and looked up. "Right on time," he said. The two men stepped aboard the boat. Washburn carried a briefcase in his hand. He handed it to Hobbs.

Oleg called down from the bridge. "I always am."

"Funny," Washburn said. "You don't strike me as the punctual type."

"You don't make much of a first impression yourself," Oleg replied. "Killing a security guard and all."

Washburn ignored him, spoke to Hobbs. "Take the case below deck. Store it someplace safe. Bring it up when I ask for it."

"Nothing comes on my boat without me knowing what it is," Oleg said to Agent Hobbs as he descended the staircase from the bridge. "Open it," he demanded. "Show me what's inside."

Hobbs looked to his partner for direction.

Washburn pointed to the stairs. Hobbs nodded, descended into the boat's galley.

Oleg became furious. He yelled at Washburn. "What part of *my boat* don't you understand?"

"Until we're done with you, this vessel is no longer *your* boat," Washburn replied. "It's the property of the U.S. government. And to satisfy your curiosity, the briefcase contains the fifty grand you negotiated to pay your friend. Happy now?"

Oleg said nothing.

"Good. Now take us out to the meet."

Oleg shook his head, climbed the staircase to the bridge, put the fishing charter into reverse, mumbled loud enough for Washburn to hear him. "Fucking feds." He shifted the *Off The Hook* into gear, then headed into open water.

IN THE DISTANCE, the Cigarette jet boat bobbed on the water and waited. Oleg slowed as he approached the craft. He called down to the agents. "That's the boat," he said. "Remember, you're supposed to be my clients, so let me do the talking. If my guy feels something's off, or you give him a reason to doubt you, he won't ask questions. He'll rabbit. If he does, you can kiss goodbye to the rest of your operation. That's a 42 Tiger, one of the fastest machines on the water. Put the hammer down on that baby and she'll reach eighty-five miles per hour in twenty seconds or less. We won't stand a chance of catching her."

Washburn nodded. "Fair enough, Mr. Schroeder."

Oleg stared at the men and smiled. "At least you both look the part. Where'd you get the clothes? You steal them from the set of a Miami-style cop show? Let me guess... you drove here in a Ferrari?"

"I suggest you pay less attention to us and more to the water," Washburn replied.

"I'm just saying. You two look like you walked straight out of central casting. I can practically hear the theme music in my head."

The pilot of the Cigarette boat raised his binoculars, inspected the oncoming boat.

Oleg turned away to not be seen talking to the agents. "He's checking us out," he said. "Time for you to act the part."

"Don't worry about us," Washburn replied. "We have everything under control."

Oleg picked up his binoculars to take a closer look at the Cigarette. "Fuck," he said.

"What is it?" Washburn asked.

"I recognize the captain but not the second guy."

"Is that a problem?"

"The Mac 10 submachine gun he's holding at his side tells me yeah, it's a fucking problem."

"Has your friend been armed when you've met with him before?"

"Of course, but with a pistol. And like I said, I don't recognize the guy holding the Mac. Never seen him before."

Washburn and his partner drew their weapons, chambered a round, held the guns at their side.

"What the hell are you doing?" Oleg asked.

"Making them aware that we're prepared to meet force with force if it comes down to it. Hopefully, it won't."

Oleg shook his head. "I should never have agreed to do this."

"You weren't given a choice."

"Don't remind me."

Oleg blasted the boat's horn once, then followed with two shorter blasts.

The Cigarette returned the nautical greeting.

Oleg neared the boat. "All right," he said. "Here we go."

The *Off The Hook* pulled up alongside the Cigarette. Oleg called out to the jet boat pilot. "Hey, Tuck. What's up?"

Ashton Tucker waved. "Just another beautiful day on the water," he replied.

Oleg nodded. "You mind telling me who your friend is? And more importantly, why he's carrying a machine gun? I wasn't expecting anyone but you."

Ashton spoke to the man in Spanish and held out his hand. The man surrendered the firearm without hesitation. Ashton placed it in a storage compartment behind the seats. "This is Mateo," Ashton replied. "He's from Cuba. He'll be providing protection for me on future runs."

"You should probably tell him that meeting a new client with a gun in his hand isn't good for business."

Ashton nodded. "We're being extra cautious these days."

"Why?"

"You know Sonny Briggs out of Staten Island?"

"Sure. He runs a charter like mine. Bigger boat, though. All of his clients are high rollers."

"He's dead. Took a family out last week to a point a few miles from here. Word is pirates killed them all, then shot up his boat. Scuba divers found it on the bottom off Long Island. It was riddled with bullet holes. People in our business are nervous. No one's picking up or transporting any new clients until those assholes have been found and taken care of. If they catch wind of our operation, they'll come after us for sure. I'm putting the brakes on everything for now. This will be my last transfer for a while."

"Thanks, Tuck. I appreciate it."

"No problem." Ashton pointed to Washburn and Hobbs. "Tell your clients to holster their weapons."

Washburn slipped his Glock into the cross-draw holster under his linen jacket. "Sorry," he said. "We were just being careful."

"No worries," Ashton replied. "I get it. It's getting harder to tell the good guys from the bad guys these days, isn't it?"

Washburn nodded. "Tell me about it."

16

"You Have A Problem."

THE FIREFIGHTERS WORKED quickly to extinguish the smoldering remains of the old couple's home. The captain spoke to the grandfather as his men doused the glowing timbers, tried to ascertain the cause of the blaze. The gentle man held his severely burned, sling-bound arm close to his chest and shook his head. He explained how the evening had begun, with him reading a book in the living room and his wife preparing tea and an evening snack while their grandson finished his homework in his upstairs bedroom. He told the fire captain how he had heard his grandson call out for him, then watched him race down the stairs in a panic. No sooner had he finished asking him what was wrong when he heard an explosion. He ran up the stairs to the boy's room where he was met by a wall of fire. When he turned away from the flames and called out to his wife, a second explosion followed the first. Acknowledging that the situation was now completely out of control, he shifted his attention from saving his home to saving his family's lives. He rushed downstairs, grabbed his wife by the arm, threw open the front door, and pushed her outside. He tried to take the same action with his grandson, but the boy resisted. A third explosion rocked the small house and sent with it shards of airborne debris. Something struck him squarely in the back of the head and dropped him to the ground. As he struggled to hold on to consciousness, he could feel his young grandson tugging at his arm, trying to pull him, but he could not. Before long, caustic black smoke had begun to fill the home. He awakened long enough to watch his grandson fall to the ground beside him, then used his remaining strength to climb on top of him in the hope of shielding him from the deadly smoke and angry fire. After that, everything went dark. The last thing he remembered was the feeling of cold water being splashed on his face and the sound of his wife's cries as she pleaded with God to let him live. Next was the sight of the strangers; two men, and a woman. His wife then explained to the captain how heroic the three had been and how the man and the woman had put themselves in danger to save the life of her husband and grandson by forcing their way into the burning building and pulling them both out to safety. When the captain asked the couple if they knew the two individuals who had performed such a courageous act, they shook their heads. No further descriptions were offered, or questions asked, except of the boy. The captain asked if they would permit him to speak to him privately, which they did. Ten minutes later, the cause of the blaze was determined. The boy had attempted to try smoking for the first time, stolen his grandfather's cigarettes and matches, opened his bedroom window to prevent the smell of smoke from entering his room, then struck the match. Never before having lit a match, its sudden ignition caught him off-guard, caused him to burn his fingers, and drop the match pack, which set off a chain reaction of catastrophic events. The blazing matches landed on the comforter on his bed, which instantaneously erupted into flame. Frozen with fear, the boy watched as the flames engulfed his wooden bed frame, climbed the wall, and raced across the ceiling. The first explosion came about as his bedroom mirror surrendered to the flames and blew out behind him. He ran from his room, calling out for his grand-father and hurrying down the stairs. He had no idea what had been responsible for the explosions which followed. The captain had all the information he needed for the moment. He chastised him, read him the proverbial riot act, and berated him for being responsible for destroying his grandparents' home. The boy's body language and uncon-trollable sobs affirmed that the remorse he was feeling was genuine and that there was nothing more he would be able to say that would make him feel any worse about what he had done. He would reiterate what he had learned to the boy's grandparents and let them take it from there. He walked the boy back to his guardians, placed his hands on the young man's shoulders, and told them what he had done. When he had finished talking, his grandmother pulled him close, told him that everything would be okay, that it was just a house, and that the most important thing was that they were all still together and alive.

His grandfather waited until his wife had finished speaking, then turned and walked away.

When they tried to follow after him, the captain suggested they give him time alone to process what he had just heard. Reluctantly, the boy's grandmother agreed.

The captain excused himself to check on his men and the scene. As he walked down the laneway, his radio crackled, and he heard his name. He answered the call and was told that he was needed at the back of the property behind the barn.

As he approached the only remaining structure on the old folk's land, he heard a cow moo, then watched two of his men step out from behind the barn, lean over, and vomit.

He rounded the corner and saw the heap of corpses piled one on top of the other. He recognized the man lying on top, covered his mouth, forced down the bile rising in his throat, then walked away from the gruesome scene, removed his cell phone from his belt, and placed a call.

The call was answered immediately. "Sí?"

"Armando, it's Luis."

"What is it?"

"You have a problem."

"What kind of problem?"

"One you need to see for yourself. Stop whatever you're doing and get over here. I'm sending you a pin now."

Armando opened the map app on his phone, saw the pin. Luis was in Sirsitara. "Give me twenty minutes," he said.

"The sooner the better," Captain Luis replied.

17

Dangerous Waters

SHTON TUCKER SMILED at his friend as the two boats bobbed beside each other on the calm water. "Sorry, Oleg," he said. "I hate to sound crass, but I believe we have a transaction to complete before we can get this party started."

"Of course," Oleg replied. He turned to Washburn and Hobbs. "Gentlemen, pay the man."

Hobbs descended the stairs to the galley, retrieved the briefcase, returned to the deck, handed the case to his partner.

Tucker leaned across the side rail of the Cigarette, extended his hand, waited for the stranger to pass him the briefcase.

Washburn held it at his side.

Tucker withdrew his arm. His pleasant disposition

suddenly changed. "Is there a problem?" he asked, a note of distrust in his voice. He glanced over his shoulder at Mateo, met his eyes. The bodyguard understood, opened the compartment between the seats where Tucker had stored the Mac 10.

Hobbs called out. "I wouldn't do that if I were you."

Mateo looked up, saw the pistol pointed at him, raised his hands.

"Step back," Hobbs ordered.

Mateo complied.

"What is this, Oleg?" Tucker asked. "Are you ripping me off? You can't be serious!"

Oleg shook his head. "Sorry, Tuck. They didn't give me a choice."

"What the fuck is that supposed to mean?"

"Exactly what he said," Washburn replied.

Tucker turned to the stranger. "Let me guess," he said. "You don't need my services."

"No," Washburn answered.

"If not that, what?"

"Information."

"What kind of information?"

"A few weeks ago, you picked up a couple out here at Mr. Schroeder's request. A man and a woman. I want to know where you took them."

"Why the hell should I tell you?"

Washburn thumbed his hand at Hobbs. "Because if you don't, my associate will put a bullet in your friend's head."

Tucker stepped in front of Mateo, motioned for the man to lower his weapon. "All right, all right," he said. "Lower the gun. There's no reason for anyone to get shot."

Washburn nodded. "My sentiment's exactly."

Hobbs maintained his position, kept his weapon leveled at the bodyguard, waited for Tucker to surrender the information they were waiting for.

"It was a ship," Tucker said.

"What kind of ship?"

Tucker spread his arms. "I don't know. A fucking big ship."

"Don't test me, Mr. Tucker. Tell me the name of the vessel."

"What does it matter? It was weeks ago. The people you're looking for could be anywhere by now."

"The name."

Tucker sighed. "It was called Goliath."

"Where was it headed?"

"Damned if I know."

"You know its name but not where it was headed?"

"Do I look like a fucking cruise director to you?" Tucker replied. "That's not what I do. I deliver people to where they need to go, and I do it under the radar. Their itinerary is none of my business. They get to their destination, and I get paid. Most of the time, we don't even talk. They sit, and I pilot the boat. That was the case here. I drove them to the Goliath, waited until they boarded the ship, then left. No champagne toast at the end of the trip, no *thanks-for-sailing-with-us-see-you-again-soon*. I'm familiar with those waters. They can be dangerous. I had no desire to stick around."

"What waters?"

"Huh?"

"You said the Goliath was traveling in dangerous waters. Where was she when you caught up with her?"

"In the main shipping lane."

"You know that route?"

"A little."

"When you left her, what would have been the nearest shipping terminal to her position?"

Tucker shrugged. "I'd be guessing."

"So guess."

"Probably Tegucigalpa, in Honduras."

"Why there?"

"Because she was fully loaded, and it's the largest port in the region. If I had to put money on it, I'd say that's where she's headed."

Washburn considered the information he had just learned, then nodded. "Thank you, Mr. Tucker," he said. "You've been quite helpful." He took the briefcase from his partner, opened it, displayed it to Tucker. "Fifty thousand dollars, as agreed. I believe you had requested small bills?"

Tucker nodded.

Washburn closed the case, secured the latches. "Catch," he said. He tossed the briefcase to Tucker.

He caught it, placed it behind his seat.

"You're not going to count it?" Washburn asked.

"Do I need to?"

Washburn smiled. "No."

"Good. Do you have any more useless questions?"

Washburn shook his head. "I don't."

"Then we're out of here."

Tucker pressed the Cigarette's ignition button. It's mighty engines roared to life.

Washburn and Hobbs watched as the jet boat executed a slow turn.

Tucker gunned the engine and purposely sprayed the men with water.

Oleg stared at the two agents. Their sopping wet linen

suits clung to them. He laughed. "Looks like Tuck got the last word." He climbed the stairs to the captain's tower, took his place at the helm.

"What a waste of fifty grand," Washburn said.

"Agreed," Hobbs replied.

Oleg started *Off The Hook's* engine and called down to the agents. "What was that?" he said. "I couldn't hear you."

Washburn looked up at Oleg. "Have you two been friends for very long?" he asked.

Oleg nodded. "Long enough. Why?"

"Shame." He turned to Hobbs. "Do it."

Hobbs removed his cell phone, placed a call.

In the distance, the Cigarette jet boat cut a perfectly straight course over the still water.

One second later, it exploded into a massive fireball.

18

Mr. Whoever-You-Are

SAVING THE LIVES of the old man and his grandson from their burning home and dealing with the gang members who had threatened to expose them had cost Matt and Kyla valuable time. They were now back on the road, and not a moment too soon.

Matt peered through the thin slits in the vegetable crate, tried to get a fix on their present location. The moonless night cloaked the road and the surrounding trees in inky darkness. Were it not for the minibus's high beams piercing through the black veil, the road ahead would have been impossible to navigate. Trees rushed past them on either side of the road as Xiomara drove as fast as he could. There were no roadside lampposts to guide them, no florescent-painted center line to define the lanes on the worn rural road.

"Where are we now?" Matt asked.

"A few miles outside of Sirsitara," Xiomara replied.

"How much further?"

"Mocorón is thirty minutes ahead. From there, it's another two hours to Rus Rus."

Matt observed Kyla staring out her window into the darkness. "You okay?" he asked.

Kyla shrugged. "I can't help thinking about the couple back there."

"What do you mean?"

"What's going to happen to them now?"

Matt shook his head. "I don't know. We helped them out the best we could. They're on their own from here."

Kyla nodded. "I know. But they're old. They're unable to defend themselves against a gang like we can."

"I know."

Xiomara joined the conversation. "One look at the couple and the Mara Salvatrucha will know there was no way the old man could have dragged their men to the back of the barn on his own, much less his wife or grandson. They'll want to know who killed them."

"What will they do to them?" Kyla asked.

"Whatever they need to do to get the answers they're looking for," Xiomara replied.

Kyla shook her head. "We shouldn't have engaged with the gang," she said. "We might just have signed their death warrant."

"You said *if* they find out about them, Xiomara," Matt said. "What do you mean by that?"

"The Mara Salvatrucha has thousands of members," Xiomara replied. "The men you killed were street soldiers, the organization's lowest of the low. The fire department will surely find their bodies in the course of their investigation. The Federal police will also be on the scene by now. The fire department will notify them of their discovery, which means the coroner's office will be called in and the bodies transported to the morgue. Once the coroner sees their tattoos and identifies them as being associated with the gang, nothing more will be done. Their bodies will be photographed and cremated, and that will be that."

"No attempt will be made to contact their families?" Kyla asked.

Xiomara shook his head. "To the authorities and the coroner's office, gang members are no different than rats. They are viewed as vermin, too high in number to make any effort to control, so they treat them as such. The unfortunate fact is that for every one of them who is killed, another will scurry up and take his place. It's a battle our government lost decades ago and is not likely to change for the better any time soon."

A phone in Matt's pocket rang. He removed it, checked the display.

"Where did you get that?" Kyla asked.

"Took it off one of the bad guys," Matt replied. "I figured he wouldn't mind if I borrowed it, what with him being dead and all. I thought it might come in handy if we needed to make a call."

"You going to answer it?"

"I don't speak Spanish."

"I do."

Matt handed Kyla the phone. "Knock yourself out."

Kyla opened the call, put the caller on speaker, said hello. "Ola."

Not recognizing her voice, the caller paused, then spoke. "Quien?"

Kyla said nothing.

Noting the American accent, the man continued in English. "Who is this?" he asked.

"Nobody you would know," Kyla replied.

"Put Emilio on the phone," the caller demanded.

"Unfortunately, Emilio can't take your call right now."

"And why is that?" the man asked.

"He's kind of dead. Can I take a message?"

"Who the fuck is this?" the caller yelled.

"Someone who doesn't care very much for assholes like your late friend."

"Did you kill him?"

"Maybe."

"You got the lady balls to tell me that, but you won't tell me you're the one who did it?"

"It's a little more complicated than it sounds."

"How so?"

"There were a lot of bullets flying around at the time. It was hard to tell the players apart. Gang members look the same. Wife-beater undershirts, prison tat's, you know what I mean. You guys really need to improve your wardrobe. Could it have been me that took out Emilio? Maybe. Guess we'll never know."

"You're American."

"To the core."

"Why did you go after my men?"

"Right place, right time."

"You have no idea what you've done."

"Oh, I think I do."

"Really? What's that?"

"Rid the world of a few more scum buckets."

"I'm going to make you regret saying that to me."

"How do you propose to do that?"

"First, I'm going to find you."

"That would be a good start. And then?"

"Kill you."

"Someone's feeling optimistic."

"That's not optimism. It's a promise."

"It's a big country. There are plenty of places for a gal like me to hide."

"Trust me, there aren't."

"We'll see."

"Do yourself a favor. Tell me where you are. I'll promise I'll kill you quickly."

"That really doesn't work for me. Besides, I've got people to see, things to do. You'd mess up my plans."

"Those plans better not include living a long and happy life. Because I guarantee that's not in your future."

"Oh, I'm pretty sure it is." Kyla heard the phone beep three times. The screen flashed a one percent low battery warning. "What a coincidence. Just like Emilio, this phone is about to die. Goodbye, Mr. Whoever-you-are."

"See you soon," the caller said.

With the caller's last words, the screen went black.

Kyla tossed the dead phone onto the seat beside her.

19

Into The Deep

OLEG HEARD THE explosion before he saw it. He swung around in his seat, saw the fireball rise into the air, watched a plume of black smoke drift up high into the sky. The water beneath the Cigarette jet boat roiled momentarily from the pressure of the briefcase bomb blast. Seconds later, the *Cerberus* and its dead passengers were absorbed into the deep.

"Jesus Christ!" Oleg yelled. He stopped the boat, brought his hands to his head in horror. "What did you do?" he cried out. "*What the FUCK did you do?*"

Washburn drew his weapon, pointed it at Oleg. "Sit down!" he ordered.

Oleg was beside himself with anger. He spat out the words. "You killed Ashton, you son of a bitch!"

Washburn discharged the weapon. The round missed Oleg by inches, ricocheted off the fishing charter's steering wheel.

Oleg jumped, lost his balance, caught himself, nearly fell from the captain's helm to the main deck below. "What's next?" he yelled. "Are you going to kill me too?" He grabbed the wheel, stood tall, puffed his chest, barked at the agents. "Go ahead, motherfucker. *Do it!*"

Washburn returned his gun to its holster. "Sit down, Mr. Schroeder. No one is going to kill you."

"Bullshit!"

"Trust me," Washburn said. "If that were my intention, you'd already be dead."

"Why the fuck did you do that?" Oleg yelled. "Ashton posed no threat to you. He gave you the information you asked for. You had no reason to kill him or his bodyguard. None!"

"I'll decide who poses a risk to this operation and who doesn't," Washburn replied. "You just do what you're told to do. Which, right now, is to drive the boat."

"And if I refuse?"

"Then my next round will go through your heart. Your left atrium, to be specific."

The rush of adrenaline that had seized Oleg as he witnessed the explosion's aftermath began to subside. Slowly, his breathing returned to normal. His hands stopped trembling. He sat in his captain's chair and stared at Washburn. "Fuck this," he said. "I'm out."

"That's not how this works, Mr. Schroeder," Washburn replied. "We're the ones dealing the cards. We tell you when the game is over. You don't tell us."

"Yeah, but I'm playing against a stacked deck."

Washburn shrugged. "What can I say? Life isn't fair."

"And if I choose to stop playing?"

"Then the agency will destroy every aspect of your life as you know it."

Oleg laughed. "You must think I'm an idiot. The second this is over, you'll do that anyway."

Washburn shook his head. "That's not true. You'll be well compensated and never have to work another day in your life."

"When were you planning on telling me that?"

Washburn smiled. "Like I said, we're holding the cards. You wouldn't expect me to play my best hand first, would you?"

"How much do you define as *richly* compensated?"

"How does two million dollars sound?"

"Like a good start."

Washburn nodded. "I'll see what I can do about bumping up that number. How much you're paid doesn't matter to me, Mr. Schroeder. It's Uncle Sam's money we're playing with, not mine."

Oleg stared at the now calm water where, moments ago, his friend had met with a horrific and fiery death. He contemplated his options, realized he had none. He turned the key, started the boat. "I want five."

"That's a substantial jump," Washburn replied.

Oleg nodded. "Yeah, it is. But like you said, it's not your money we're playing with. It's Uncle Sam's. If he can afford to blow up fifty grand, he can sure as hell pay me five mil for my help."

Washburn smiled. "I couldn't agree with you more."

"Good," Oleg replied. "So, where to from here?"

"Back to the government dock where you picked us up.

We need to change into dry clothes. After that, drive your boat back to the marina and stay there. I'll touch base with you again in a few days."

"You'll have my money then?"

"I'll need to get approval for that high an amount, but I'm sure it won't be a problem. Would you prefer we deposit it into your account?"

Oleg shook his head. "Thanks, but I'll take it in good old-fashioned U.S. cash."

"Let me guess... small denominations, nothing bigger than a fifty?"

Oleg smiled. "It's like you can read my mind."

Washburn nodded. "As you wish."

Oleg increased power to the boat's engine. The *Off The Hook's* bow rose out of the water, then lowered as the craft settled into a gentle plane. The fishing charter skimmed across the glassy surface. One hour later, it reached the waterfront government dock adjacent to the former site of Red Thunder Fireworks.

The agents stepped off the boat. As Hobbs headed for their car, Washburn turned and looked up at Oleg. "Remember what I said. Stay on the boat. We have to go out of town for a few days. Don't leave the marina. If you need something, have it delivered to the slip. Keep a bag packed and wait for my call. Be ready to leave at a moment's notice."

"Where will I be going?" Oleg asked.

"Probably nowhere. It's just a precaution."

Oleg nodded. "All right."

Agent Washburn watched as the *Off The Hook* left the dock and headed into open water. He removed his phone and placed a call.

Director Ferriman answered. "Yes?"

"It's Washburn, sir. We have a lead on Gamble and Reese."

"Is it credible?"

"I believe so."

"Then follow it. Whatever resources you need, you have them. Just one thing."

"What's that, sir?"

"There's been a development. A directive has been issued. The capture/kill order on Gamble and Reese has been rescinded. You're to bring them in alive."

"That might not be so easy, sir. Gamble has a reputation. So does Reese. They both tend to shoot first and ask questions later."

"Then make sure you get the drop on them. Let me make this very clear, Agent Washburn. If Gamble is killed, there will be repercussions. Do you understand?"

"Yes, sir. We'll take care of it."

"Good. Now tell me about this lead."

"We believe they're in Honduras."

"Take the Lear," Ferriman replied. "I'll call the hangar and have it prepped for takeoff. It'll be ready when you arrive at the airport."

"Thank you, sir."

"One last thing."

"Sir?"

"This is a high-value, make-or-break assignment. I strongly recommend you don't screw it up."

"Understood, sir."

Ferriman ended the call.

Washburn met Hobbs at the car. "So?" Hobbs asked. "Where to?"

"First, we change."

"And then?"

"Pack a bag. We're going to Honduras."

"What about Schroeder?"

"We'll deal with him later."

Hobbs nodded. "Copy that."

20

A Very Nice Man

AS HE STEPPED out of his car at the scene of the fire, Armando Canales ended the phone call with the American woman who had just informed him that one of his most reliable street soldiers, Emilio Fuentes, was dead. Around him, emergency personnel tended to their responsibilities. Police officers held back curious neighbors behind a wooden barricade and directed what minimal traffic the under-traveled road received past the site of the devastating blaze while fire officials doused the smoking embers to extinguish any threat of a subsequent eruption.

Fire Captain Luis Gonzales walked up the driveway, met Armando at his car. The Mara Salvatrucha gang leader spoke to him. "What's so important that I needed to come here right away, Luis?"

"There's something you need to see," Luis replied solemnly.

"It better be more important than a burned-down house."

"It is. At the back of the house. Behind the barn."

"Lead the way," Armando said.

"You might want to prepare yourself for what I'm about to show you, Armando," Luis said as they walked to the end of the driveway and reached the barn. He pointed. "There, around back."

Armando stepped around the corner, saw the stack of dead bodies piled high atop one another. Emilio's dead eyes stared back at him. Unlike the police and firefighters who had been unable to stomach the grisly sight, he walked up to the pile and pulled one body off the other. Armando took out his phone, snapped pictures of the deceased, returned the phone to his pocket. He turned to the fire captain. "Who did this to my men?" he asked.

Lost for words and shocked at the gang leaders' nonplussed reaction to the mass carnage, Luis hesitated, then spoke. "I don't know. We found them here like this. I recognized Emilio, so I called you right away."

"You did the right thing," Armando said, then opened his blazer pocket. He pulled out an envelope full of cash and handed it to the fire chief.

Luis looked over his shoulder, waited until no one was looking, then quickly pocketed the money. "Thank you, Armando," he said.

"Were you and your men the first to arrive?" Armando asked as he circled the bodies, inspecting them closely.

"Si."

"Who was here?"

Luis pointed to the old couple and the boy standing beside the smoldering rubble, talking to the police. "Just the homeowners and their grandson."

"Have they talked to anyone other than the police?"

Luis shook his head. "No one that I saw."

"I want to talk to them."

"Shouldn't you wait until the police have completed their interview?"

Armando stared coldly at Luis. "What do you think?"

Luis understood. "Of course," he said. "I'll take care of it right away."

From a distance came the wail of an ambulance siren. Seconds later, it pulled in behind Armando's white Mercedes AMG GT Roadster. The paramedics exited the vehicle, grabbed their supply packs, and jogged down the driveway where the police met them. After briefly inspecting the burn, they began to treat the old man's arm.

Luis walked over to the policeman standing with the family, whispered in his ear, pointed at Armando.

The officer nodded, told the paramedics to excuse themselves.

As the men walked away, Luis accompanied the family to the barn.

Armando said his final goodbyes to his men, crossed himself, then walked to the barn. He stood silently, staring at the couple and their grandson, then spoke. "Do you know who I am?" he asked.

The old man stepped forward, met the gang leader's cold stare. "I know who you are, cabrón. You are El Diablo, the Devil, and I want you off my property now."

Armando smiled, stepped away from the man, walked to the double doors leading into the barn, lifted up the long wooden board which kept them closed, and tossed it aside. He swung open the large doors and walked inside.

An old car stood beside a flatbed truck.

"Inside," Armando said.

The family and the fire captain entered the barn.

Armando glanced at Luis, gestured toward the door. "Close it," he said.

Luis complied with the request.

Armando walked to the flatbed, opened the driver's door, peered inside, removed a picture taped to the sun visor, closed the door, and returned to the couple. "Is that your truck?" he asked.

The family said nothing.

"It isn't," Armando said. "Do you know why I know that?"

"Leave," the old man said. "Don't make me ask you again."

Armando showed the photograph to the family. "The man in this picture worked for me," he said. "The woman holding the baby on her lap? His wife and child. His is one of the bodies lying on the ground behind your barn. So before you think of threatening me again, let me make a suggestion." Armando stepped forward, grabbed the boy, pulled him away from his grandparents. He withdrew a gold-plated Sig Sauer pistol from his waistband and pressed it against the boy's temple.

"Teo!" his grandmother cried. "No!"

The old man grabbed his wife's arm as she lurched forward to grab young Teo. "He won't shoot him," he said.

"Why wouldn't I?" Armando replied.

"Because if you do, we'll never tell you what you want to know."

Armando looked at Luis and smiled. "What do you think, Luis?" he asked, chambering a round. "Should we put that theory to the test?"

"There's no reason to kill the boy, Armando," Luis replied.

Armando returned his attention to the boy's grandparents. "I'm not so sure about that."

"Two of them were American," Teo blurted out. "They saved me and my grandpa from the fire!"

Armando pressed the gun harder against the boy's head. "Go on."

Teo grimaced as the weapon's front sight pierced his skin. The cut drew blood. He felt its warmth as it trickled down his cheek.

"They came out of nowhere," Teo's grandmother cried. "We don't know who they are. Our home was on fire, and they were driving towards me, so I waved them down. They helped us. I don't know how or why, but they shot your men, then dragged their bodies behind the barn. That's all we know. I swear!"

"How many were there?" Armando asked.

"Three."

Armando turned to the boy. "You said two of them were American, not three?"

Teo nodded. "Sí. The third man was from here. I've seen him before. He travels this road many times."

"Do you know him?"

"Sort of."

"What do you mean?"

"I know him by the little bus he drives."

"Little bus?"

"Sí. Once in a while, he sees me playing at the end of our

driveway. He'll stop and give me free vegetables. He's a very nice man."

"Did he tell you his name?"

Teo hesitated.

"Tell me his name, boy," Armando said. He pressed the muzzle of his weapon hard against Teo's temple.

Teo winced. "His name is Xiomara."

21

Ghost

MATT GLANCED AT Kyla and smiled. "Well, that went well," he said, referring to her phone call with the unknown man. "Look at you, making friends everywhere you go."

"Yeah," Kyla replied. "I'm a real people person."

"It sounded like you touched a nerve with that guy."

Kyla nodded. "I'm pretty sure he'd like to see me hanging from a bridge right about now."

"That would be for starters," Matt replied. "Down here, guys like him make their point with machetes."

"Thanks for the visual."

Xiomara spoke. "I think I recognized his voice."

"You did?" Kyla asked. "Who was it?"

"Armando Canales. The leader of Mara Salvatrucha."

"You know him?" Matt asked.

"Not personally," Xiomara replied, "Like I said before, I used to get stopped by the gangs all the time. Since I converted my minibus to appear like I'm transporting fruits and vegetables to market, they don't bother me anymore. On the rare occasions when they stop me, I get out of the van first and start handing out food. That's the routine now. You could almost say I've become friends with some of them. I remember one occasion when they stopped me. They had blocked the road, as they are known to do. A car was parked on the side of the road. It was beautiful, a white Mercedes. A man stood beside it, talking to the gang. He was impeccably dressed. You could tell that his clothes were expensive, as was his car. I heard him speaking. He had a very distinct voice, smooth and melodic. I remember it because it sounded like Carlos Moncada, a famous Honduran actor. The man on the phone sounded very much like him."

"Are you telling me that the top guy in Mara Salvatrucha just threatened me?" Kyla asked.

Xiomara nodded. "It would seem so."

"Well, that's just perfect."

"Don't worry about it," Matt said. "He has no idea who you are or where you are, and you'll never talk to him again. The phone's dead, so he can't track its GPS to determine our location. To him, you're a ghost."

"That may not be as simple as you make it sound," Xiomara said.

"What do you mean?" Matt asked.

"Here, in Honduras, we believe in ghosts," Xiomara replied. "Besides, you've poked the hornet's nest by talking to him the way you did. I heard it in his voice. He already knows enough about you to put your life in danger. He knows you're an American, that you're a woman, that you admitted to killing his men, and that you may or may not be working alone. Phone or no phone, you can be sure that Canales has already begun to reach out to his network of connections. It's now more important than ever that the two of you stay out of sight. I've learned enough about gang life to know what will happen next. He'll put a bounty on you with a number high enough to make everyone stop what they're doing and start looking for you. He'll want you taken alive. What you said before about your body swinging from a bridge isn't far from the truth. Whichever end he chooses for you, he'll make an example out of you. If there is one unwritten law here that everyone knows and respects, it is that no one disrespects the Mara Salvatrucha. That includes the police and politicians."

"Where does that leave us?"

"In quite a predicament, I'm afraid," Xiomara replied. "Had it been me, and not you, I would never have answered that phone."

"Unfortunately, we're past that now," Kyla said.

Xiomara nodded. "We are indeed."

"What do you think, Xiomara?" Matt asked. "Is there any point in us continuing to Rus Rus? Won't we be in as much danger there as we are here?"

Xiomara shook his head. "I don't think so. I've been there many times. Rus Rus is too rural for the Mara Salvatrucha to bother with. I have never seen a gang member there. The people of Rus Rus are so independent they're probably the only ones I can think of who would not be afraid to stand up to them. Most of its residents have lived there for generations. Their ancestry dates back to the sixteenth century and the days of the Paya, Mayan, and

Sumo. They have warrior blood running through their veins."

"If that's the case, won't they object to the presence of outsiders, especially Americans?" Matt asked.

"I'm not an outsider," Kyla stated. "To them, I'm a friend."

"You don't know if the people you once knew are still there," Matt said. "What if we go there and no one recognizes you? We'll have made the trip for nothing."

"Do you have a better idea?" Kyla asked.

Matt thought for a moment. "No, I don't."

"Then we have our answer."

"I guess we do."

"Rus Rus it is."

To Xiomara, Matt said, "You heard the lady."

Xiomara smiled. "Yes, sir. I did."

In the distance, bright lights illuminated the turn ahead. A car raced through the corner, then accelerated toward them. Blinded by its high beams, Xiomara slowed the minibus, hugged the shoulder of the road, gave the oncoming vehicle plenty of room to pass, waited for it to whiz by, then pulled back onto the road. In his rearview mirror, he watched the car speed down the road. "Something doesn't feel right," he said.

"What doesn't?" Matt asked.

"That car that just passed us."

"You recognize it?"

Xiomara shook his head. "No."

"Then what?"

"I don't know. It just gave me a bad feeling."

Far behind them, nearly out of sight, Xiomara watched as the speeding vehicle suddenly applied its brakes. The bright red lights lit up the road. The car swung from right to left. Its high beams illuminated the dense forest as the driver executed a three-point turn.

"He's turning around," Xiomara said. "Hold on."

Xiomara put his foot to the floor, buried the accelerator pedal. The minibus rocketed forward, took the turn at speed. The crates behind Matt toppled over, spilling their contents over the floor.

"What is it?" Kyla asked. "What's wrong?"

Xiomara tried to hide the fear in his voice. "It's the Mara Salvatrucha," he replied. "I don't know how but they've found us."

22

Teterboro

THE AGENCY'S LEARJET 75 sat on the tarmac outside its secure hangar at New York City's Teterboro Airport, fueled and ready for the flight to Tegucigalpa, Honduras. Washburn and Hobbs arrived at the main gate, received authorization from the armed guards to enter the facility, drove their cars to the jet, boarded the aircraft, took their seats, and buckled in. The jet's powerful engines whined as it taxied along the runway to its designated departure point. Seconds later, its twin Honeywell turbines roared to life. As it accelerated along the runway, the thrust of its mighty engines pressed the agents back into their seats. Washburn stared out the window as the aircraft rocketed skyward, then watched it bank sharply, leaving New York City's coastline behind, and began to follow its programmed flight path southwest over the Atlantic Ocean.

Hours from now, they would be on the ground in Honduras and one step closer to fulfilling their assignment to bring in Gamble and Reese alive.

It was the *alive* aspect of the mission that concerned Washburn. He shared Ferriman's update with his partner.

"He knows who we're dealing with, right?" Hobbs said. "If Gamble or Reese recognize us, they'll take us out the first chance they get. I don't know Gamble, but from what I've heard of his reputation, he's not the kind of guy who'll meet us with a friendly smile. He's well aware of the predicament he's in. And if he's still with Reese, they're together for a reason. His instinct will be to protect her at all costs. That makes him dangerous and unpredictable."

Washburn nodded. "I know."

"Did Ferriman mention anything about providing us with additional backup once we're on the ground?"

Washburn shook his head. "We're it."

"It might be two against two," Hobbs said, "but I still don't like the odds."

"Why is that?" Washburn asked.

"Think about where we're going. If you were in their position and wanted to disappear, would you choose Honduras?"

"Not for a damn second. The place is dangerous as hell."

"Which means only one thing."

"What's that?"

"That either Gamble or Reese know someone there who can hide them, or they know of a place that's so off the radar they're confident they'll never be found."

"As far as *places* go, you just described ninety percent of the country."

"Which is why Ferriman should have provided us with

additional assets. This operation requires a team, not just the two of us. We'll be lucky if we catch a lead, much less find them."

"It's too late now," Washburn replied. "As far as the team goes, you're looking at it. We better come up with a workable plan."

"You have something in mind?"

"Maybe."

"What?"

"You ever heard of the gang named MS-13?"

"The Mara Salvatrucha? Of course. They're one of the most powerful gangs in the U.S. Their numbers are in the thousands."

"They're not just located in the States. They're across all of Mexico and Central America, including Honduras. I think we might be able to use them to our advantage."

"How?"

"When we arrive, we'll need to contact a senior player in the gang and ask him to put the word out about Gamble and Reese and let the Mara Salvatrucha find them for us. Like you said, we need a team. They could be it."

"Think they'll agree to it?"

Washburn nodded. "If we offer a sizeable bounty for Gamble and Reese's safe capture and return to us they will."

"How much are you thinking?"

"That can be negotiated."

"So we let them do the grunt work while we sit back and wait."

"Exactly. Besides, who knows better where to look for Gamble and Reese on their home turf than the Mara Salvatrucha?"

Hobbs nodded his agreement. "No one."

"If we handle this properly," Washburn continued, "we could have them on the jet and heading back to the U.S. within a day or two. A week, tops."

Hobbs smiled. "It's a good plan. I like it."

"A good plan with one small caveat."

"What's that?"

"We'll need to find the right MS-13 person to work with in Honduras. Someone with a great deal of pull. Ideally, a member of the Council of Nine."

"Council of Nine?" Hobbs asked.

"They're the top of the MS-13 hierarchy," Washburn explained. "They make the decisions and pass down orders to their cell leaders."

"How do you propose we find out who that would be?"

"We ask."

"Who?"

"Someone in the National Police Force, perhaps. They have a reputation for being corrupt. Word is the MS-13 has them in their pocket. If we can connect with the right cops and pay them enough, they should be able to arrange a meeting for us pretty fast. Five hundred dollars should do it. To a National cop, that's a small fortune."

"There's still the matter of bringing in Gamble and Reese."

Washburn nodded. "They might be good, but they're no match against a small army like the Mara Salvatrucha. They'll be outnumbered and outgunned. After we have them, I'll ask the leader to have his men provide us with an escort back to the airport. Gamble and Reese won't be going anywhere except back home."

"What about Ferriman?"

"What about him?"

"You think he'll approve the idea?"

"I don't plan to tell him about it."

"We could be overstepping our authority here."

Washburn smiled. "I prefer to look at it as thinking outside of the box. This is the optimal operational solution that offers the best chance for a successful conclusion. Besides, Ferriman isn't the one in-country. We are. Not to mention, we're the fucking CIA. We make up the rules as we go along, remember?"

"Damn straight."

"Then it's settled," Washburn said. "We have a plan."

"What about the information we got from Schroeder's late friend Tucker?"

"You mean about the Goliath?"

"Yeah."

"We'll have the Mara Salvatrucha look into it. If there's anything worth following up on, they'll tell us. We'll take it from there."

Washburn pressed the recline button on his seat back. The chair slowly fell back into an outstretched, comfortable position.

"We have a few hours before we land," he said. "Better get some rest. We'll hit the ground running in the morning."

Hobbs nodded, reclined his chair. "Good plan."

23

This Should Cover It

CANALES LOWERED HIS gun and released the boy. Teo ran into his grandmother's arms. She leaned over, inspected the wound created by the pressure of the weapon's front sight against Teo's temple. The cut was small, nothing to be concerned about. The bleeding had stopped. She turned on the gang leader, screamed at him. "*Diablo!*"

Armando smiled.

"We've told you everything we know," Teo's grandfather said. "You have no further reason to be here. Leave, now!"

Armando returned the gun to his waistband, walked past the frightened family, threw open the barn doors. "I'll decide when it's time to leave, old man," he replied. "In the meantime, stay out of my way." He pointed his finger at the fire captain. "Come with me."

Captain Luis nodded, followed him out of the barn.

The scene had become busier since Armando had ushered the old couple and their grandson into the barn and begun his interrogation. Together with Captain Luis's men, National Police officers scoured the grounds in search of evidence. Upon seeing Armando, the officers stopped what they were doing. Armando waved his hand. "Carry on," he said. The men and women resumed their duties.

One of the officers approached Armando, spoke to him. "Excuse me, Señor Canales?"

Armando stared at him. "What is it?"

The officer opened his hand. "We found these scattered about. Some were on the road, others in the driveway."

Armando picked up one of the shell casings, inspected it closely. "How many did you find?" he asked.

"Six."

"That's all?"

"Sí."

Armando dropped the casing into the officer's hand. "There must be more," he said. "Keep looking."

The officer nodded, walked up the driveway, panned his flashlight across the ground, continued searching.

"You seem concerned, Armando," Luis said.

"I am."

"About?"

Armando returned to the back of the barn, stared at the dead bodies of his street soldiers. "My men are highly trained," he replied. "They carry plenty of firepower, both assault rifles and handguns. Yet here they lay."

"Sí," Captain Luis replied. "It is unfortunate, to say the least."

"There can be only one explanation for what happened here," Armando stated.

"What is that?"

"They never saw it coming. Or when they did, it happened so fast they had no time to react."

"You're thinking they were ambushed?"

Armando nodded.

"Who would do this?" Luis asked. "Everyone knows to cross the Mara Salvatrucha means an immediate death sentence."

"Apparently, someone doesn't."

"I can't think of anyone who would be so bold."

"I can," Armando replied. "The Americans the boy spoke of. And the vegetable vendor."

"Three of them against all your men?" Luis shook his head. "That seems unlikely."

"Not if they're professionals."

"You think someone is coming after the Mara Salvatrucha?"

Armando nodded. "The policía have recovered six casings so far, all of them small caliber, nine millimeter. Which means they were fired from a handgun. If my men had had time to react, they would have fanned out and sprayed the grounds with automatic weapons fire. The road and driveway would have been littered with brass and bodies, yet it's not. Whoever took them out did so quickly and with extreme precision. Only a professional would possess the skill to make each round a kill shot, whether the shot was taken from a distance or at close quarters."

Armando and Luis watched as two police officers walked past them, entered the barn, and inspected the flatbed truck his men had driven. One of the officers instructed the family to leave the barn while his partner climbed into the cab, started the engine, and drove the vehicle out and onto the driveway. When he was clear of the doors, he stopped, put the truck in Park, exited the cab, and called out to his men for assistance. No one responded. He called out again, forcefully this time, and pointed to the back of the barn. Reluctantly, several officers acknowledged his request and joined him while two additional policemen climbed into the truck's cargo bed, unfurled a crumpled plastic tarp, laid it out, dropped the tailgate, and waited.

The officers worked in pairs, carrying the dead bodies from behind the barn to the flatbed, where they tossed them unceremoniously up and onto the tailgate. Their fellow officers grabbed the corpses, dragged them forward to make room for the next, then placed one beside the other, organizing the space as best they could until all the bodies lay in the back of the truck.

Armando was furious. He yelled at the officer in charge. "Why are you putting them in there? Where is the coroner's hearse? Their remains should be respected. You're treating them like garbage you're taking to the dump!"

The officer nervously replied. "I apologize, Señor Canales. We would never intentionally disrespect you or your men. I spoke to the coroner and explained the situation to him. He suggested we make use of the flatbed. There are only two ambulances and one hearse for the entire region; both ambulances are currently in service and unavailable. There are simply too many bodies for one hearse. We are only doing what we have been instructed to do."

Armando shook his head in dismay. "All right," he said. "Carry on."

The officer nodded. "Thank you, Señor."

Armando walked over to the family, yelled at them. "You know more than you're telling me!"

The old man shook his head. "No, we don't."

Armando removed the Sig Sauer pistol from his waistband, tapped its barrel impatiently against his leg. "Yes, you do," he replied.

"We *don't*," the old man insisted. "Like we said, we've never seen them before. They appeared out of nowhere, pulled my grandson and me out of the fire, battled with your men, then left."

"Describe the Americans to me."

The old man shrugged. "There were two of them, a man and a woman, both Caucasian, mid-thirties, good looking, but in a rugged sort of way. When they engaged with your men, they did so like they were accustomed to dealing with such situations."

"Meaning?"

"The way they moved. They didn't appear to be nervous at all. They moved with intent, tactically. Your men fell quickly. The gunfire was over as fast as it had begun."

"And the vegetable man?"

"I didn't see him fire a weapon. Then again, we were trying to stay hidden to avoid the gunfire. We watched everything from a distance. When it was over, the American backed the truck into our barn, then the three of them left in the minibus."

"Where were they headed?"

The old man pointed. "West, toward Sirsitara."

"Describe the minibus. What did it look like?"

"Like a *minibus*. They all look the same to me. It was dark, and they'd parked on the road. Like the rest of me, my eyes are old. I don't see well at night anymore. But it shouldn't be too hard to find."

"Why is that?"

"Because it's the only minibus I've ever seen on this road."

Armando paused, searched the man's eyes for the truth, believed him. Satisfied, he put away the gun, slipped his hand into his pocket, and pulled out a large wad of bills secured with an elastic band. He placed the money in the man's hand.

"What is this for?" the old man asked.

"You'll need a new house. This should cover it."

The old man tossed the money on the ground. "Keep it," he replied. "We don't want your charity."

"Look around you, old man," Armando said. "Everything you have is gone. You need money now more than you've ever needed it in your life."

"Not yours, we don't."

"You'd rather be homeless and on the street?"

"If it means not being in your debt, yes."

Armando turned his back on the family, called out as he left them standing in their driveway. "Then that makes you not just old and frail but stupid. Pick up the money and take care of your family. It means nothing to me. I've already made it back." He walked to his car, climbed behind the wheel, closed the door, removed his cell phone, and placed a call.

"Sí?"

"It's me. I need you to do something right away."

"Of course. What is it?"

"Text everyone. Tell them to search the area."

"For?"

"A minibus. It was last seen leaving Puerto Lempira heading toward Sirsitara."

"And if they find it?"

"Stop it. Detain its passengers, then call me immediately."

The man replied. "I'll send the text right away."

Armando ended the call, tossed the phone into the vehicle's center console, and hit the gas. The Mercedes tires spun on the loose dirt, then bit into the road. The car accelerated.

Sirsitara awaited.

24

Locked and Loaded

MATT GLANCED OVER his shoulder, peered through the slits in the vegetable crate, searched for the vehicle which had taken chase before they had taken the turn in the road, saw nothing. The road behind them remained dark. He spoke to Xiomara. "Think we can beat them to Mocorón?"

Xiomara shook his head. "There are only a few more turns ahead. After that, the road opens up for a mile before the next turn. Once we're there they'll see us for sure. To be honest, I've never driven this minibus this fast before. It's an old vehicle. I hope it doesn't overheat!"

"Then we don't have a choice," Matt said.

"What do you mean?" Xiomara asked.

Kyla spoke. "He means we need to switch vehicles; the sooner the better."

"Where am I supposed to find another vehicle out here?" Xiomara objected. "We're in the middle of nowhere!"

"You aren't," Matt said. "We let it come to us."

Xiomara shook his head. "If you're suggesting what I think you are, I don't like that idea at all."

"Neither do I," Matt replied. "But if the word is already out about us and the minibus, we need to get control over the situation right now. Keep watching the road. The second you see a place to pull over, do it, then jump out and pop the hood. Put on your hazard lights. Make it look like you're having engine trouble. When the car comes into view, wave them down and ask for help."

"What are you going to do?" Xiomara asked.

"I'll leave that decision up to them," Matt said. He turned to Kyla. "As soon as we're out of the minibus, find cover. Remember our whistle?"

Kyla smiled. "Copy that. One long, two short."

"You got it."

"I see a spot up ahead," Xiomara said. "We won't have much time. Their vehicle is much faster than mine. They'll be on us in seconds."

"Take it," Matt said.

"Hold on!" Xiomara replied. He targeted the spot, drove the minibus off the road, then slammed the brake pedal to the floor. The front passenger tire caught the edge of a narrow ditch. The sudden stop on the uneven surface caused the vehicle to tip precariously to the right before gravity reclaimed it. The minibus fell back down on all four tires. Xiomara called out. "Everyone okay?"

"I'm good," Kyla replied. "Compared to a Humvee, this is a Cadillac."

"Same," Matt replied.

Xiomara threw open his door, exited the minibus, then opened Matt's door.

Matt and Kyla hurried out of the hidden compartment. Matt grabbed two of the assault rifles he had taken from the dead gang members at the old couple's property, handed one to Kyla. The two operatives inspected the weapons, checked the clips, made them battle ready.

"I've got a full mag," Matt said. "You?"

Kyla removed the clip from her AR-15, inspected it, slammed it back into place, racked a round. "Locked and loaded."

"Good," Matt said. He glanced down the road.

In the distance, the treetops glowed.

Headlights.

"They're coming," Matt said. He turned to Xiomara. "We'll take cover across the road. Get the minibus ready."

Xiomara watched them disappear behind the tree line, turned on his emergency hazard lights, released the lock latch, then hurried to the front of the van and raised the hood.

Matt could see he was terrified. He called out. "Don't worry, Xiomara. You've got nothing to worry about. You'll be fine. We've got your back."

"It's not just my back I'm worried about," Xiomara replied. "It's my head, my neck, my arms, my legs... my everything!"

Matt tried to calm him. "Like you said, you're just a vegetable vendor, remember? You pose no threat to them."

"When all of this is over, that is exactly what I'll be from now on. No more secret rides for anybody!"

"Fair enough," Matt replied.

The vehicle's headlights exploded out of the darkness as the car sped up the road towards the minibus.

Xiomara took a few deep breaths, said a prayer, crossed himself, then stepped onto the road.

Matt and Kyla watched as he waved his arms.

The chase car turned off its high beams, slowed, and stopped behind the minibus.

Three men exited the vehicle, guns drawn. The driver yelled out. "On your knees!"

Xiomara complied with the gunman's order. "Don't shoot!" he cried. He lowered his head, stared at the ground, pointed to the van. "Please," he said. "I have a family. I have no money, just vegetables. Take all you want! Just don't kill me!"

25

Contingency

OLEG SCHROEDER EASED *Off The Hook* into its slip at the Marine Basin Marina, cut the engine, secured the vessel's mooring lines, then glanced at the parking lot. The lot, which had been a beehive of police activity when he had left to pick up the operatives, was now filled with cars, including John Simmons's prized Porsche 911 GT3 RS; evidence that the police detectives and forensics teams who had been scouring the scene earlier had completed their investigation of the area. Ribbons of red and black crime scene tape hung from the security booth. He thought about Earl, the guard, and how his life had been taken in such a matter-of-fact manner by the same men who, just a few short hours ago, had handed an explosives-packed briefcase to his friend and detonated it seconds later, obliterating him, his boat, and his bodyguard. Washburn had made it clear that he was to stay put and not leave the *Off The Hook*, that he would be back in touch with him shortly when he had secured the five million in cash which he had demanded.

Five million dollars.

Oleg descended the stairs into the galley, grabbed the bottle of single malt he had reserved for a special occasion, and cracked it open. He took a long, greedy swig, followed by another, then set the bottle on the counter and closed his eyes. The liquid burned his throat as it went down, a penance he accepted without objection. He attacked the bottle again and again until the alcohol took effect. He walked to the dining table, sat on the wooden bench seat, placed the bottle in front of him, and took stock of his predicament. How the hell had his life come to this? Everything he had ever loved or treasured was gone. Instead of picking up the pieces of his shattered life and moving on as he should have done, he'd chosen to follow a path of self-destruction.

The death of his wife had been the trigger.

No, not her death. Her *murder*. Death had merely been the result.

It was his fault, and he knew it. He should have been there. He could have done something, *anything*, to stop it. Couldn't he?

No, that wasn't true.

The alcohol began to do its job. It clouded his mind, fed his guilt, and summoned ghosts from his past.

Another unwise swig, followed by a heavy sigh. Oleg drummed his fingertips on the tabletop.

Five *million* dollars.

No, it wasn't worth it. Not five million, not ten, not even twenty.

He knew what would happen if he waited for the agents to return. They would continue to string him along, offering him more and more money until he was no longer of value to them. Then, they would find a way to get rid of him, just like they had Ashton Tucker.

Oleg stopped the bottle, returned it to the shelf, hurried to the bow, entered the boat's stateroom, opened the closet door, removed a small suitcase, and tossed it onto the bed. He pulled the few articles of clothing he kept on board off their hangers, shoved them into the case, and carried it to the foot of the stairs. He returned to the kitchen bench seat, which served double duty as a storage bin, lifted it, and removed his computer from its bag, along with the hidden satchel of money. He powered up the device, logged in, and checked the balances in his three numbered escape accounts in Geneva, Grand Cayman, and Dubai. All funds were accounted for. The operatives and their boss had not done as deep a dive into him as he thought they had, which meant he still had an advantage over them, albeit a small one.

He could do what they would never expect him to do.

Run.

Oleg always suspected that he would be forced to make such a decision one day, and it had nothing to do with his present situation. The people and organizations with whom he had conducted his clandestine business dealings over the past five years were, at the very least, unpredictable, but more accurately, ruthless. He had been reminded on too many occasions by cartel drug lords and mafia bosses alike how his life would come to an end faster than he could ever imagine should he inform on them. Knowing this, he had set up the accounts as a contingency plan should he ever feel the need to make a quick escape. That need never felt as great as it did at this very moment.

Oleg walked up the stairs, stepped onto the deck, and looked around. The evening was dark and quiet. He descended the stairs, grabbed his rolling suitcase, computer bag, and money satchel, then locked the galley door, stepped off the boat onto the pier, and walked out of the parking lot.

The Jag was parked two blocks away. Oleg arrived at his car and examined his rear right tire. The crushed plastic water bottle cap, which he had retrieved from the ground beside the car when he'd parked it and wedged under the tire, was exactly where he had placed it, evidence that no one had moved the car in his absence. He knew that by taking such a precaution he was probably being paranoid, but sometimes the line between paranoia and precaution was a fine one. He walked around the vehicle, knelt, examined its undercarriage. Nothing looked out of place. However, if someone had planted an explosive device under his car, he probably wouldn't have recognized it. Boats were his thing, not cars.

Oleg popped the trunk, placed the bag of money, his suitcase, and the computer bag side by side in the compartment, closed the lid, unlocked the driver's door with the electronic key fob, took his place behind the wheel, started the car, then breathed a sigh of relief when it did not explode. He was safe.

He turned on the car stereo, pressed SCAN, and let his mood to choose the music for the hour-long drive to the airport. He settled on light jazz and pulled away from the curb.

John Simmons had once mentioned that Switzerland was quite beautiful at this time of the year.

Oleg decided to treat himself to a night at an expensive hotel on the airport strip. In the morning, he would bound for Geneva.

The CIA could screw itself.

26

Friends and Guns

WASHBURN AND HOBBS stared out the window of the Learjet 75 and watched the Honduran coastline come into view. The aircraft banked sharply and descended into Ramón Villeda Morales International Airport. Once the jet had reached its designated hangar, the agents gathered their flight bags and disembarked the plane. They were met on the tarmac by a strikingly beautiful young woman. She introduced herself to the two operatives.

"Agents Washburn and Hobbs?" the woman asked.

Washburn replied. "I'm Washburn. And you are?"

"Grace Poncaya, operations officer, Honduras station. Director Ferriman informed our station chief you were inbound. I've been asked to provide whatever you need relative to your assignment while you're in the country."

Washburn checked his watch. It was late. The day had been long. "Can you recommend a decent hotel?"

"Of course," Poncaya replied. "The Interborough in San Pedro Sula. It's a few minutes from here. I'll take you there."

"Sounds perfect."

The operatives followed the officer to her car. She popped the hatch on the Lincoln Navigator. The men tossed their bags into the cargo hold.

"I have welcome gifts for you," Poncaya said. She handed each man a brushed aluminum briefcase.

Washburn and Hobbs opened the cases. "Nice choice," Washburn said.

Hobbs nodded. "Agreed."

Washburn removed a leather cross-draw holster from his case, slipped into it, then withdrew the Glock semiautomatic pistol, ejected the clip, checked its capacity, full, then slipped the magazine back into the weapon and fitted it into the holster.

Poncaya watched the men rig up. "You should know that here in Honduras, there are two things you can never have too many of," she said.

"What's that?" Washburn asked.

Poncaya winked. "Friends and guns. And not necessarily in that order."

Washburn smiled. "Anything else?"

Poncaya removed a manilla envelope from the hatch, handed it to him. "Down here, we call this a conversation starter."

Washburn opened the envelope and fanned the stack of U.S. currency. "How much?" he asked.

"Fifty thousand."

"That won't be enough."

"I know. Thus, the card."

Washburn looked inside the envelope, withdrew the special card. It was black, with an oval circle in the upper right corner. "A ghost card?"

Poncaya nodded. "Call the number on the back if you need to transfer funds to an account. It has no withdrawal limit, and no password is required. That being said, please use it conservatively." She withdrew her cell phone, entered a PIN code, then attached a scanning device to her phone's power port and passed the ghost card's magnetic stripe through the reader. The oval outline on the black card glowed bright red.

"Place your thumb in the oval," she instructed.

Washburn placed his thumb on the card, watched as the oval's color turned green.

"That's it," Poncaya said. "Your all set. Your biometric signature has been assigned to your card. It can be used by no one but you."

Washburn slipped the card into his pocket. "Thanks for the goodies," he said.

The agent smiled. "Don't thank me. Thank the U.S. government."

Washburn grinned. "My tax dollars at work, huh?"

Poncaya nodded. "Exactly. You two ready to roll?"

"Yeah."

"Then let's mount up," Poncaya said, then walked to her car.

PONCAYA PULLED into the Interborough Hotel and parked beneath the portico outside the main entrance. "Here we are," she said. She exited the vehicle and waited for the men to retrieve their belongings, then handed them each a slip of paper. "My number, in case you need it, although something tells me you won't."

Washburn nodded. "We have a plan. It's not exactly on the book with agency protocol, but I've never been one to follow the rules."

Poncaya smiled. "I get that impression."

"Question for you."

"Shoot."

"If we wanted to make a new best friend in the Mara Salvatrucha, someone high up, who would you suggest we talk to?"

"You'll need to be vetted first. MS-13 doesn't exactly have an open-door policy when it comes to exposing their leaders to strangers, especially American CIA operatives. You'll need to buy your way into a meeting as a show of good faith, and that won't come cheap."

Washburn smiled. "Sounds like my ghost card will be getting a workout."

"Yes, it will. There is a man in Tegucigalpa, a former director of the National Police Force. His name is Juan Cabral. It's common knowledge he's in tight with the Mara Salvatrucha."

"Is he a member of the Council of Nine?"

Poncaya shrugged. "Could be. I'm not sure. Our intel on him is limited."

Washburn nodded. "One last thing."

"What's that?"

"We'll need wheels."

Poncaya nodded. "I'll have a car delivered to the hotel by morning. Don't expect anything fancy. Down here, the last thing you want is to be conspicuous. If you're driving a flashy car, and not a gang member, the MS-13 will kill you for it in a heartbeat."

"Good to know."

"What can I say? Welcome to Honduras. Try not to get into too much trouble while you're here."

Washburn smiled. "Oh, I'm sure we will."

"I'm serious. When you're in the city, watch your six. Foreigners are targets down here. It's common to see American tour groups accompanied by armed bodyguards."

"Personally," Washburn said, "I'd prefer to skip the city tour and crash on a beach."

Poncaya smiled. "Can't blame you. Oh, I just remembered. Cabral owns a nightclub in Tegucigalpa. It's called the Lima Lounge. He frequents the place. You'll probably find him there."

Washburn nodded. "Will do. Thanks."

Poncaya called out as she walked to her car. "Call me if you need me," she said, then slipped behind the wheel and drove off.

The men entered the hotel.

Tomorrow was going to be a busy day.

With any luck, they'd find Gamble and Reese quickly and wrap up their assignment early.

And Juan Cabral would become a rich man for helping them.

27

Tight Space

"WHERE ARE THEY?" the gunman yelled. Flanked by his two associates, he leaned over, pressed the muzzle of his pistol hard against the back of Xiomara's head.

Xiomara winced, pleaded. "They? I don't know what you're talking about! My van broke down. I thought you were stopping to help me! Please, I have no money to give you, only vegetables. Open my van. You'll see. Take it all. Just let me live. I have a wife and daughter."

Whistling sounds, first one, then another, emanated from the forest across the road.

The gunman looked at the tree line. He stood, placed his foot on Xiomara's back, pinned him down, then turned to his men. "What was that?"

The first man shrugged. "What was what?"

"Those whistles."

"Birds?" the second man asked.

The gunman shook his head. "Not at this hour." He pointed across the road at the dense forest and gave them an order: "I'll deal with the vegetable man. You two check it out."

"You want us to look for a *whistle*?" the first man asked.

The gunman did not reply. He raised his finger, motioned for them to be quiet, listened intently as he searched the trees.

Nothing moved.

He continued. "Find out what it is."

The second man glanced at the third, pointed. "You go up the road. I'll start down here. We'll meet in the middle."

The third man nodded, raised his weapon, crossed the road, entered the thicket.

"There's a flashlight in the car," the gunman said. "Get it, use it."

The second man shook his head. "No need," he replied. "I can see like a hawk in the dark. If there's something in there, I'll find it. Besides, I still think what you heard were birds."

"Did I ask you for your opinion?" the gunman said.

"No."

"Then don't give it."

"Sorry." He chambered a round, then crossed the road and entered the forest.

The gunman pushed Xiomara with his foot, then stepped away from him. "On your feet," he demanded.

Xiomara stood, brushed specs of dirt and gravel off his shirt and pants. "Thank you," he said.

"For what?" the gunman asked.

"Not shooting me."

"Yet."

"What?"

"For not shooting you *yet*."

Xiomara raised his hands. "I'm no threat to you."

"What are you doing here?"

"I have produce to take to market, fresh vegetables," Xiomara replied. He pointed to the rear door of the minibus. "See for yourself."

The gunman kept his weapon trained on Xiomara as he walked to the back of the vehicle and opened the rear cargo doors. Two crates toppled out of the bus. Their contents rolled across the road.

Peppers and squash.

The gunman kicked away the produce. He turned on Xiomara. "You're lying to me. I can tell."

Xiomara raised his hands. "I'm not! I swear! I have no reason to lie to you!"

The gunman glanced across the road and called out. "Sanchez!"

The second man failed to respond.

"Sanchez, where are you?"

Silence.

"Gonzales!"

No reply.

The gunman was furious. He ran to Xiomara, wrapped his arm around his neck, pressed his gun against his temple, yelled. "Who's out there? Come out now, or he dies!"

A single shot rang out from inside the black veiled forest. The round caught the gunman squarely in his choke arm, shattering his radius and ulna, and blowing out his elbow joint. He screamed, dropped the gun. As Xiomara ran for cover behind the back of the van, a second round followed the first. The gunman wheeled around as the bullet tore through his left scapula, then ricocheted off his clavicle and obliterated his use of both arms. He fell against the van and slid to the ground, broken and bleeding.

Matt and Kyla emerged from the dark forest, each dragging a gang member with them. They deposited the dead bodies on the ground beside the wounded gunman.

"Of all the lowlife guerrilla wannabes in this country," Matt said, "you'd think you guys would learn a thing or two about jungle warfare." He tossed the length of thick vine he had used to surprise and strangle the man to death on the ground.

Kyla was more direct. "I wasn't as resourceful as my partner," she said. "I just broke his neck. Quick and painless. For me, that is. For him... not so much."

The gunman raised his head and stared at Matt and Kyla. "Who are you? What are you doing here?"

"We're honeymooners," Kyla replied. "Can't you tell?"

The gunman looked up at Kyla, then spat on the ground at her feet. "Fucking puta!"

"How rude," Kyla said. She turned to Matt. "He just called me a whore. Are you going to let him talk to me like that?"

"Not for a second," Matt replied. He knelt beside the gunman, grabbed the man's near-dead arm, twisted it as hard as he could.

The man cried out in pain.

"Apologize to the lady," Matt said.

"Fuck you!"

"Your body is in rough shape," Matt said. "Which is good because that's exactly what I was going for. Even if you're lucky enough to get to a hospital within the next hour, chances are you'll bleed out, or go into shock on the way. However, if by some act of God you happen to make it to one, even the best surgical team on the planet won't be able to save this arm. Like you, it's done. So maybe I should save you the trouble of worrying about how you're going to navigate the rest of your life without it and rip it off you right now. Does that sound like a plan?"

The man's breathing had become erratic. "I think I'm dying," he said.

"I guarantee you are," Matt replied. "That's the bad news. The good news is that I know how to stem the bleeding and save your life and maybe even your arm. You want me to do that?"

The gunman hesitated, then nodded.

"Good," Matt said. "First, apologize."

The gunman looked up at Kyla, spoke faintly. "I... apologize."

"Apology accepted," Kyla replied.

"You're Mara Salvatrucha?" Matt asked. "MS-13?"

The man nodded.

"Who do you work for?"

The man said nothing.

Matt turned his arm, watched him grimace.

"Armando!" he cried out. "Armando Canales!"

Matt glanced over at Xiomara. "The same guy Kyla spoke to earlier?"

Xiomara nodded. "Yes. He's a clica leader for the Mara Salvatrucha, a very dangerous man. The locals call him El Diablo, the Devil. They even named this part of Sirsitara after him. They call it Devil's Road."

Matt turned his attention back to the gunman. "Did he send you after us?"

The gunman shook his head.

"No? Then why come after us?"

"We got a text telling us to watch out for a minibus and to stop it if we found it, then contact Armando." The gunman tried to laugh, choked instead. "Looks like we found the right minibus."

"What does Canales want with us?"

"What do you think?" the gunman replied. "You killed his men. He wants to kill you."

"Leave him, Matt," Kyla said. "He's dying anyway."

"You have a phone?" Matt asked the gunman.

The man nodded.

"Where is it?"

"Back pocket."

Matt retrieved the phone. "Use your good hand to call Canales. Tell him where you are and that you need help."

"If he finds me like this, I'm a dead man."

"No, you're not. I'll stem the wound and slow the bleeding. That will give you an hour, maybe two. After that, your clock runs out."

The gunman nodded. "All right."

Matt raced into the forest, retrieved several lengths of ropey vine, and tied off the man's wounds as best he could. He pulled him to his feet. "Get in the bus," he ordered.

The man groaned as he struggled to stand. Kyla slid open the bus's side panel door, then the secret compartment. "Get inside," Matt said.

The gunman stared at the tight space. "You want me to get in *there*?"

"You have two choices," Matt replied. "Do it yourself, or

I'll fold you in half and shove you inside. First, make the call. Tell your boss you found the van. And don't try anything stupid. My partner speaks fluent Spanish. Tell Canales anything other than where you are and I'll open you up. You'll bleed out in a minute. Got it?"

The gunman nodded, then shuffled into the compartment. "You're wasting your time," he said. "Canales is a resourceful man. He'll find you. And when he does, you'll wish you'd never set foot in Honduras."

"Newsflash, pal," Matt replied as he searched the man's pockets and relieved him of his car keys. "I've felt that way from the second I got here."

Matt, Kyla, and Xiomara listened as the gunman placed the call, informed Canales of his location, then ended the call. He had not said anything to put them in any greater danger than they were already in.

Matt warned the gunman as he closed the door to the secret compartment. "Don't even think about trying to escape. Move your arms the wrong way and you'll spring a leak. Comprendes, amigo?"

The man nodded.

Matt held up the car keys, jangled them. "We'll be taking your wheels. Hope you don't mind."

The gunman stared at Matt and shook his head. "You're all dead. You just don't know it yet."

"We'll see," Matt replied. He closed the secret compartment, then slammed shut the minibus door.

"What do you want to do with these two?" Kyla asked.

Matt opened the bus's rear doors, lifted the bodies, tossed them on top of the produce crates. "They can keep our friend company until his boss arrives." He closed the doors, tossed Xiomara the keys to the gang members car. "Get us out of here," he said.

Together they ran to the late model Trans Am, jumped in.

"Don't stop for anyone or anything until we reach Rus Rus, Xiomara," Matt said. "Got it?"

Xiomara started the car, dropped it into gear, punched the gas. "Got it."

28

Thump

ARMANDO CANALES HEARD the fear in his enforcer's voice. The call had been brief. He and his men had found the van. Shots had been fired. No mention was made as to whether it was the Americans who had engaged with them or rival gang members. All he knew at this point was that the situation was dire, that his men were in trouble, and that he needed to get to them as quickly as possible.

The tires of the Mercedes AMG GT Roadster bit into the asphalt as it negotiated the tight turn. Armando raced the car through the nondescript town of Sirsitara, then gunned the engine when he reached a long straightaway. He turned on his high beams as he pulled through a turn in the road, then saw it ahead, in the darkness, parked on the shoulder of the road.

A minibus.

Armando brought the car to a stop, stared at the vehicle. The Mercedes emitted a throaty growl as it idled on the dark road.

Something felt wrong.

Armando retrieved his phone from the center console, checked his most recent call, called the number, and listened while it went to voicemail. He stepped out of his car, walked up the road, tried the number again. The ring volume was faint, but he was able to determine its location.

It was coming from inside the minibus.

Armando ended the call, pulled his gold-plated handgun from his waistband, chambered a round, returned to his car, removed a flashlight from the glove compartment, turned it on, and cautiously approached the minibus.

The vehicle was devoid of rear and side windows, which made seeing into it impossible, other than through its front windshield. Armando moved carefully, panning the surrounding forest and the bus with the flashlight. He tilted the beam high and low, checked around and under the vehicle, then advanced to the front of the bus. He crept ahead, shone the beam inside the minibus, up, down, side-to-side, illuminated the interior. No one occupied the passenger cabin of the vehicle. The area behind the cab appeared to be full of crates.

Satisfied he was not at risk of being ambushed by a gunman hiding in the front seat of the bus, he decided to clear the vehicle. He grabbed the side door handle, used it for cover as he slid it open, then searched the interior with the flashlight.

In front of him were crates, all stocked with fresh vegetables.

As the flashlight beam reached the back of the van, it fell upon the deceased bodies of his men.

Armando walked to the back of the bus, opened the rear cargo doors, and cast the light over the men.

Sanchez lay on top of Gonzales. He inspected the bodies, found no blood. The men had not been shot. He looked for further signs of trauma, found it.

Their necks had been broken.

These men were not incapable of defending themselves. Sanchez had made his mark in MS-13 as a reliable hitman, with dozens of kills to his credit. Gonzales was a newer member of his operation but as reliable.

There was no doubt in his mind that whoever had murdered his men had to be a trained professional.

Could it have been the woman he had spoken to on the phone? No, that was impossible. These were fit, well-muscled men. Surely, they would have been able to defend themselves against a woman. The old man had mentioned that two individuals had rescued his family from the fire which had taken their home and who had subsequently murdered his men. They had to be working together. Armando felt a rage building inside him. The death toll was rising, and he was powerless to stop it. Somewhere out there were the two Americans and the vegetable man, and they were taking his people out, one by one.

But it was Cruz who had called him, not Sanchez or Gonzales. His body was not in the back of the minibus with the dead.

Had he wandered off, tried to find help, and collapsed by the side of the road?

Armando tucked his gun into his waistband and the

flashlight into his back pocket. He removed his cell phone and redialed the number.

As before, the phone rang. His hearing had not deceived him. The sound *was* coming from inside the minibus.

He shoved the dead bodies aside, searched for Cruz beneath them, found nothing.

Then he heard it. A groaning sound, low and faint, followed by a muffled knock.

Thump.

Armando drew his weapon as fast as he could, trained it inside the minibus, called out. "Cruz?"

Thump.

He zeroed in on the sound. It was coming from beneath the crates. He ran to the side of the minibus, searched for the source of the sound, then heard the thumping sound again. It was right in front of him.

Armando tossed the crates out of the minibus, exposed the door to the secret compartment, yanked it open.

Fernando Cruz lay slumped in the confined space.

"What the hell?" Armando said, shocked at the sight.

Cruz stared at his boss and spoke. His words were barely audible in his near-death state. "Help... me."

Armando reached into the compartment, grabbed his enforcer by his blood-soaked shirt, dragged him out of the minibus. Fernando screamed as the thin vine the American had tied above his bicep slipped down and grated against his exposed tendons and ligaments. A jolt of pain surged through his body like an electric shock and threatened to render him unconscious. He fought against the desire to surrender to it and concentrated on Armando's voice.

"What happened?" Armando said. "Who did this?"

Fernando stared at his boss. He slurred the word. "Mercans."

Armando understood. "The Americans?"

Fernando nodded.

"They killed Gonzales and Sanchez too?"

Another weak nod.

Armando punched the side of the minibus. "Puta's! Were they alone?"

Fernando shook his head.

"Who was with them?"

"Dunno."

Armando looked around the minibus, saw the produce scattered around the back of the vehicle. "The vegetable man?"

Fernando nodded. "Vegebbleman... drivver."

"The vegetable man was the driver?"

Another nod.

"Where did they go?"

Fernando shook his head. "Took... car."

"They took your car?"

Fernando nodded, licked his lips. "Need... hsspittle."

"You'll never make it to a hospital," Armando said. "You've lost too much blood. You'll die on the way."

Fernando reached out, pulled on Armando's sleeve. "Try... please."

Armando stood. Fernando's hand fell slack and struck the ground at his side. The MS-13 leader stared down at him. "This is on you, Fernando. You let this happen."

Too weak to look up, Fernando shook his head.

"No? You see anyone else here who isn't dead besides me?"

"Nvvr..."

"Never what?"

"Saw it... coming."

"Then that makes you sloppy."

Fernando shook his head. "Nuuuh."

"You let your men get killed. Soldiers I put you in charge of. Good men. *My* men."

A bloody string of spittle fell from Fernando's mouth and touched the ground. "Hsspittle," he repeated.

"Sorry, Fernando," Armando said. "No hospital for you." He drew his gun from his waistband, pressed the muzzle against the dying man's skull, pulled the trigger.

Fernando's body jumped in unison with the expended round, then fell on its side.

The hitman was dead.

Armando spoke to the corpse. "No chance I'm getting blood on my interior, asshole," he said. "I just got the car detailed." He opened the driver's door, hopped into the minibus, began rifling through the center console, checked the sun visors, then opened the glove box. The small compartment was packed with invoices, gas receipts, maps, candy bar wrappers, and assorted papers. Armando examined each item, tossed aside anything he deemed unimportant, and then stopped when he found what he was looking for. He read aloud the information on the vehicle's insurance slip. "Xiomara Castillo, Puerto Lempira. So that's who you are, Mr. Vegetable Man." He shoved the paper into his pocket, continued rifling through the glove box, found a family photo. A man, whom he assumed to be Xiomara, stood beside his wife and daughter. He recognized the background in the photo as the main fishing pier in Puerto Lempira. Armando removed his cell phone, snapped a picture of the insurance papers which bore Xiomara's home address and the photo of him standing with his family, then placed a call.

"Sí?"

"It's me."

"Sí, Armando," the man said. "What do you need?"

"Remember the broadcast text you sent earlier?"

"Sí."

"Cancel it. We're no longer looking for a minibus. Tell everyone to be on the lookout for a black Trans Am with furry dice hanging from the rearview mirror."

"That sounds like Fernando's car."

"It is. Or should I say, it was. He's dead. The Americans took it."

"I'll send the message right away."

"There's one more thing I need you to do, and I want you to take care of it personally."

"Of course."

"I'm texting you a family photo and the address of a man in Puerto Lempira. His name is Xiomara Castillo. I believe he's involved with the American's. I want you to go to his village, find his wife and daughter, and bring them to me."

"I'll take care of it right away."

"Good. Let me know as soon as you have them. We'll arrange a place to meet."

Armando ended the call, then walked down the road to his Mercedes. When he reached the car, he opened his door carefully and removed a bottle of water from the center console. He walked to the front of the car, examined his hands and Gucci loafers in the headlights, then removed a handkerchief from his pant pocket, dampened it with bottled water, wiped clean his hands and the soles of his shoes. He threw away the soiled handkerchief, seated himself behind the wheel, took a swig of the water, then drove past the death scene.

In the morning, he would find the vegetable man and the Americans.

When he did, he would take his time killing them.

29

VIP

WASHBURN AND HOBBS awoke early the following morning, geared up, and checked out of the Interborough Hotel. The desk clerk handed Washburn a set of car keys. "For you, Señor," she said. "A vehicle was delivered to the hotel for you late last night. We thought it best not to call your room for fear of disturbing you. I hope that was okay."

Washburn accepted the keys. "Of course," he said. "Thank you for being so considerate."

The clerk smiled. "De nada," she said. "I trust everything was to your liking?"

"It was," Washburn replied. He looked around the lobby. "Where can I grab a coffee?"

The clerk handed him his receipt, pointed to her left.

"Our guest lounge and breakfast bar are around the corner. We offer coffee and pastries. Please help yourself."

"Perfect."

"Is there anything else I can do for you this morning?"

"There is," Washburn said. "We're driving to Tegucigalpa. I'll need a map if you have one, as well as directions."

The clerk opened a drawer in front of her, pulled out a paper map, laid it out in front of the two men. Using a highlighter, she traced a route from the hotel to the capital city. "This is the most direct route," she said. "The traffic should be fairly light right now."

"How long will it take to get there?" Hobbs asked.

"Four hours, maybe less," the clerk replied. "Just watch your speed. The National police like to pull over speeders. They'll decide on the spot how much your fine will be and demand you pay them in cash, which is never an insignificant amount. I'm sorry, but that's how things work here in Honduras."

Hobbs nodded. "We've been warned about the corruption and how to conduct ourselves."

"I wish that were not the case," the clerk said. "But unfortunately, it is."

Washburn jangled the car keys in his hand. Two keys. One for the ignition, one for the trunk. Grace Poncaya wasn't kidding when she'd said not to expect anything fancy regarding their mode of transportation. He wondered what make and model of vehicle awaited them in the parking lot. A cardboard tag attached to the keychain bore the vehicle's license plate number: P BD 4699.

Hobbs thanked the clerk, folded the map, and slipped it under his arm.

The men grabbed a coffee and a snack for the road and left the hotel. Although it was early morning, heat radiated off the asphalt as they crossed the parking lot. They located the vehicle Poncaya had provided for them.

Washburn stared at the late model Hyundai Avante, confirmed its plate with the number on the tag affixed to the keychain. "You've got to be kidding me," he said. He set his cup on the roof, walked around the vehicle, and picked at the rust eating through its wheel wells and trunk lid. "This thing looks like it's ready to fall apart."

"Look on the bright side," Hobbs said. "It has dark tinted windows."

Washburn inserted the key into the lock, unlocked the door, peeked inside. "There's dark, and there's *dark*. I can barely see out."

"That could be a good thing."

"How so?"

"If no one can see inside, they won't know we're Americans. Which means there's less chance of us being stopped." He smiled. "That is, as long as you don't speed."

Washburn shook his head. "Funny guy." The men walked to the back of the car and tossed their overnight bags in the trunk. Washburn closed the trunk. "Guess we better get rolling."

Hobbs nodded.

Washburn retrieved his coffee from the roof, slipped behind the wheel, started the car. The engine idled quietly. "That's a good start," he said.

"My grandfather had one of these," Hobbs said. "He thought it was great."

Washburn dropped the car into gear and pulled out of

the parking spot. "I guess we're going to find out just how great it is."

Hobbs placed his coffee cup into the drink holder, unfolded the map, bit into the powdered cinnamon donut he had helped himself to from the breakfast bar, took a bite. "Looft," he said as they exited the hotel parking lot.

"What?"

"Hang a looft."

"You mean *left*?"

Hobbs nodded, took another bite of the donut. "Thas wha I said. Looft."

"Do me a favor?"

Hobbs glanced at his partner. "Wha...?"

"Don't navigate with your mouth full."

Hobbs smiled, took a swig of his coffee, swallowed the remains of the donut. "Sorry," he said. "My bad."

FOUR HOURS LATER, the operatives reached the congested capital city of Tegucigalpa. Pedestrians swarmed the road, interrupted traffic. Children selling bottles of water and fruit converged on the car, banging on the roof as they inched their way through the downtown core, yelling at the men to buy their goods or give them money. Twenty minutes later, Hobbs pointed to a street sign. "There it is," he said. "Hang a right at the lights."

Washburn rounded the corner and saw a sign on the building ahead: LIMA LOUNGE. He pulled the car into a parking space and shut off the engine.

The men observed the building.

"Nothing curious about that, is there?" Washburn said.

"About what?" Hobbs asked.

Washburn pointed. "Check out the roof."

Hobbs looked up and noted the two men positioned on the rooftop, one at either end of the building. "Would you wear a jacket on a day as hot as today?" he asked.

"Only if was concealing a weapon," Washburn replied.

"Precisely. Think that's their daily post?"

"Possibly." Washburn glanced in his rearview mirror and watched as a black Land Rover rounded the corner. "Well, what have we here?" he said.

"What is it?"

"Hold on. I'll bet you any money..."

The Land Rover stopped in front of the Lima Lounge. The entrance door to the business opened. Three well-muscled men dressed in business suits stepped out of the building. As the first man opened the car door, the second and third took up positions at the front and rear of the car. The bodyguards opened their jackets and studied the street.

"They're armed," Washburn said. "Must be a VIP who's arriving."

"Yeah," Hobbs replied. "And I'll bet I can guess who it is."

Washburn nodded. "Juan Cabral."

"There's only one way to find out if that's him."

"Yep."

"You ready?"

"As I'll ever be," Washburn replied. He opened his door, stepped to the back of the car, and opened the trunk.

Washburn and Hobbs's sudden exit from their vehicle caught the attention of the rear bodyguard. The man's hand whipped to his waist as he watched the Avante's trunk lid rise. He drew his weapon, pointed it at Washburn, yelled. "Hands where I can see them!"

Washburn raised his hands, followed by Hobbs.

The Land Rover passenger glanced at the two men staring down the barrel of his bodyguard's gun. Unfazed by the sudden commotion, he entered the Lima Lounge.

30

Belle Epique

OLEG PLACED THE soiled dinner plate, cutlery, and cloth napkin on the room service catering cart, rolled it outside his hotel room door, glanced up and down the hallway, then closed and locked the door. He had no idea why he suddenly felt nervous. He had no reason to be. To his knowledge he had not been followed after he had left the marina and navigated a random route to the Hilton hotel where he had booked a night in a luxury suite. He returned to the bed, propped up his pillows, lay back, turned on the television, and watched the morning news. Being so close to the airport, the hotel offered two channels that provided up-to-the-minute flight information for the convenience of its domestic and international traveling guests. Oleg waited for the screen to scroll to Swiss Airlines information. His flight time from JFK to Geneva hadn't changed. Later this afternoon, he would be bound for the Swiss capital and the start of a new adventure. He would miss the United States. It was his home. However, his current circumstances dictated the need for an immediate departure. Perhaps one day he would no longer be seen as a priority for the CIA or feel the need to look over his shoulder every minute of the day. The situation with Ashton Tucker had unnerved him, made him fear for his life. If they could blow up a total stranger, his boat, and his bodyguard after a single meeting, what would they do to someone whose information they valued? Oleg knew he was thinking irrationally, that in the greater scheme of things he was not *that* important to them. He wasn't exactly a spy. He had information on two people the agency needed to reacquire: nothing more, nothing less. Certainly, that was not worth his life. There had to be plenty of other citizens the covert agency would be better off directing its efforts to find than him.

A knock on the door drew his attention away from the television. He rose from his bed, tightened his robe, put on his slippers, walked to the door, looked through the peephole.

A pretty brunette stood outside the door. Oleg opened it.

"Mr. Schroeder?" the woman asked.

"That's me," Oleg replied.

"I'm Connie, from Red Rose Massage. You booked an appointment with me?"

Oleg smiled. "Yes, I did. Please, come in."

Connie rolled her portable massage table through the door into the spacious suite. "My," she said. "This is beautiful."

"It is, isn't it?"

"One of the nicest I've seen on the strip." She looked around the room. "Where would you like me to set up?"

"Anywhere is fine," Oleg replied.

"There is one small matter we need to discuss before we begin," Connie said. "I hope you don't mind."

"What's that?"

"The nature of my business."

"Meaning?"

"I'm a licensed professional massage therapist, Mr. Schroeder. Red Rose Massage is my company. I don't offer... how shall I put it... *other* services."

Oleg smiled. "That's quite all right, Connie. I'm just looking for a good old-fashioned get-the-knots-out massage. Rest assured I won't be asking you for anything else."

Connie looked relieved. "Good," she said. "Unfortunately, some clients do expect more." She pointed to the lounge area. "I can set up in front of the window if you'd like."

"That would be fine."

Within a minute Connie had set up the massage table, covered it with a clean sheet, invited Oleg to lie face down and make himself comfortable, then draped his body with a blanket to keep him warm.

Last night, after checking into his room and helping himself to several bottles of Scotch from the room's minibar, he fired up his computer, searched *things to see and do in Geneva* as well as *most affordable places to live*, and made a list. First, he would get a Geneva Pass which would grant him free access to many places of cultural interest in and around the city. Next, he would take a day cruise on Lake Geneva, explore Yviore Castle and the Olympic Museum at Lausanne, then walk the cobblestone streets of Vielle Ville.

A day trip to Chamonix, complete with cable car and train ride, was also a must.

Oleg let out a heavy sigh as he settled in for his massage. He allowed his body to relax and his mind to wander as Connie worked her magic on his tense and tired body. Within minutes, he fell asleep.

In his dream, he boarded the Belle Epique sightseeing tour boat from the Swiss bank and enjoyed the stops along the Geneva-Nyon-Lausanne cruise as the vessel navigated Lake Geneva's calm waters for the next three and a half hours. The breathtaking views of the castles, vineyards, and Alps from the many harbors reinforced his decision that fleeing the United States was the smart thing to do. John Simmons had been right. Switzerland was a beautiful country. As the captain announced the tour was ending and the boat would be returning to its home port, Oleg suddenly felt unsettled. A strange feeling came over him. He looked skyward and watched as the perfectly blue and sunny day began to change. The puffy white clouds which had offered a magnificent backdrop to the idyllic landscape turned grey. The sky began to rumble. Lightning streaked across the heavens, followed by a tremendous boom. One by one, the sightseers left the deck of the boat as fat raindrops fell from the sky. Oleg thought it best to follow their lead and head inside to the safety of the dining room, but his feet would not move. He tried to lift them but couldn't. He called for help, but as loud as he yelled his voice could not be heard. The heavy droplets had now morphed into Swiss francs. Oleg covered his head as the coins fell on him, clinking as they bounced on the ships steel deck. Before long, he was waist deep in coins. Their sheer weight caused the boat to list. Terrified passengers screamed, ran to the opposite side, tried to level the vessel with their cumulative weight, couldn't. The ship began to sink. Oleg fell into the water, swam as far away from the doomed vessel as he could. When he'd reached a safe distance, he looked up into the sky. What he saw took his breath away. It was his own image, reflected against the roiling clouds. He recognized the scene from the previous evening. He was seated at the desk in his suite, checking the balance in his Swiss account, pleased with himself for having stashed away six million tax free dollars. But now the balance was dropping, faster and faster with every second, until soon no money remained in his account. When the balance reached zero, the coins stopped falling. As Lake Geneva claimed the boat and the many souls that had been its passengers, the sun broke through the clouds. Oleg found himself stranded and alone, treading water, far from shore. Sailboats drifted past him, oblivious to his life-threatening situation. He heard their passengers laughing and chatting as they sailed by. Suddenly the meaning of dream sent him reeling back to consciousness.

As though having received a massive electric shock, Oleg's body jumped on the massage table. He cried out.

Taken aback by her client's sudden and violent reaction, Connie stepped away from the table. "Are you all right, sir?" she asked.

Oleg took a second to get his bearings, saw he was in his hotel room.

Connie handed him his bath robe. "You don't look well, Mr. Schroeder," she said. "Would you like me to call the hotel doctor?"

Oleg took a deep breath, smiled at the masseuse. "I'm fine. My apologies. I guess I fell asleep."

Connie smiled. "No worries. It happens. Are you sure you're okay? Can I get you anything? A glass of water perhaps?"

Oleg shook his head. "No, thank you. I'm good now." He

stood. "This is probably a good time for us to wrap up our session."

Connie smiled. "No problem. Just give me a minute to pack up."

"Take all the time you need," Oleg replied.

Oleg thought about the nightmare and it's possible meaning. Fleeing to Geneva could turn out to be a grave financial mistake. It might even cost him his life.

He saw Connie to the door, tipped her generously, then opened his computer, canceled his flight and hotel reservation, and packed his bags.

He would return to the *Hook*, wait to be contacted by the agents, collect the five million he had asked for, then leave the country for good.

Oleg walked to his hotel window, looked outside. The bright morning sky had turned grey. The sun had taken cover behind malignant clouds. A flash of lightning lit up the heavens, followed by a low rumble.

A storm was moving in.

31

No One Is A Stranger

ATT AND KYLA awoke to the sounds of the surrounding jungle. Matt cracked his window, looked up, and watched as a flock of scarlet macaw flew from tree to tree above him. Still asleep, Xiomara sat behind the steering wheel, his head slumped against the Trans Am's side window. He snored quietly. Matt stretched out as best he could in the confine of the front seat. He glanced over his shoulder at Kyla. "You sleep okay?" he asked.

When they arrived at the outskirts of Rus Rus the previous evening, Kyla had suggested they wait until morning to enter the village. Matt had agreed. Xiomara drove the Trans Am down an unused road less than a mile from the tiny village. He and Matt covered the car with tree branches which camouflaged it from the road and made it impossible to see against the inky backdrop of the forest.

The sound of their voices awakened Xiomara. He glanced at Matt, watched as he opened his door to step outside, then grabbed his arm.

Matt stared at Xiomara. "What the hell?"

"Don't you dare leave this car by yourself!" Xiomara warned.

"I need to take a leak," Matt replied. He tried the door again.

Xiomara held his arm. "Not without me, you're not," he replied.

Matt stared at him. "Really, it's okay. I can do it on my own. I've been peeing by myself for years, even gotten the hang of it now. Pardon the pun."

"That's not what I meant."

"Then what?"

"If we leave this car, we do so together and bring guns. You can pee while Kyla and I watch your back."

"Is this some kind of weird Honduran custom?" Matt asked.

Xiomara smiled, shook his head. "Hardly," he replied. "We might only be a hundred feet or so from the road, but we're still in the jungle. There's a reason why the people who live here rarely venture out after dark or before sunrise, and then only in pairs, armed with flashlights and weapons."

"Why's that?"

"Cats, snakes, and spiders. Jaguar and puma, to be specific, plus pit vipers and tarantulas. This area is thick with them. Not to mention crocodiles. We're less than a mile from the periphery of the rainforest. As far as wild places go, this is as wild as it gets."

"Point taken," Matt said. "Tell you what. I'll let you go first. Let me know if the coast is clear."

Xiomara smiled. "We go together, or you hold it. Your choice."

Kyla sat up, grabbed her gun, patted Matt on his shoulder. "Come on, big boy," she said. She opened her door and stepped outside the car. "Let's get that rascal squared away."

Matt and Xiomara opened their doors. Xiomara spoke quietly. "Shh," he said. "Be quiet." He walked behind the TransAm. "Matt, cover my back. Kyla, cover Matt's." He raised his gun, pointed it into the shadow-filled forest.

"I thought you don't like guns," Matt said, noticing the weapon in Xiomara's hand as he relieved himself. When he had finished, he removed his weapon from the small of his back, scanned the treetops and surrounding forest for signs of movement, saw none. "I'm good," he said. "Your turn."

"No, I don't like guns," Xiomara replied, "but I like the thought of being attacked by a jaguar or puma even less."

Matt spoke. "Go for it, Kyla."

Kyla scoffed. "Oh, please. Me, pee in front of you two? Thanks very much but I'll wait."

Matt chuckled. "Suit yourself," he said. "Come on. Let's clear the car and get out of here."

KYLA SPOKE to Xiomara as he drove the Trans Am into the tiny village. "There," she said. "That's the hospital I spoke of. Park the car around back."

Xiomara followed her instructions.

Matt stepped out of the vehicle. "Are you sure we're safe here?" he asked.

"We're safer here than anywhere else in Honduras," Kyla replied.

"That's assuming your friends are still here and they're willing to hide us."

Kyla nodded. "Guess we're about to find out, aren't we?"

Matt pulled his shirttail over his pants, covered the weapon tucked into his waistband. "Guess we are."

"Let's try the hospital first," Kyla said. "It might be open, or it might not."

"Who ever heard of a hospital that's *not* open?" Matt said.

"Remember where you are. This is Rus Rus, not New York," Kyla replied. "Last time I was here, there were three doctors for every thousand people living in Honduras. Most of the families I knew relied mostly on herbal medicines and homemade tinctures as their main means of medical treatment."

The trio stepped around the hospital, made their way to the front entrance. Kyla tried the door.

Locked.

A voice called out from behind them. "You need help, Señora?"

Kyla turned to see an elderly woman walking towards her. "Thank you, but we're fine," she said. "Perhaps you can help me in another way. I'm looking for an old friend. His name is Alvaro Marroquin. Do you know where I might find him?"

The old lady took Kyla's hand in hers. "I'm sorry, dear," she said. "Alvaro died a year ago."

"Oh my," Kyla said. "That's terrible news. May I ask how?"

"Drugs," the woman replied.

Kyla was surprised. "Alvaro never struck me as the type who would take drugs."

"Take them? Heaven's no. He was shot and killed by a drug dealer."

"Why?"

"For standing up to him when he tried to sell drugs to his son. The dealer pulled out his gun and shot him on the spot. He died at his son's feet."

"My god!" Kyla replied. "Poor Cesar. Did the police arrest the drug dealer?"

The woman smiled weakly. "There are no police around here."

Matt stepped forward. "May I ask what happened to the boy?"

The woman crossed herself. "He took him."

"Who took him?"

"The drug dealer. Cesar hasn't been seen to this day."

"Did he have a mother?"

The old woman nodded. "Sí. Maria."

"Did she try to find him?"

The woman shook her head. "She knew better than to try."

Matt was speechless.

The woman looked them over. "When was the last time you had something to eat?" she asked.

No one replied.

"Ah," the woman said. "You are too proud to say." She wagged her finger. "That will not do. You are in my village now, and in Rus Rus no one is a stranger. Please, you must come to my home and let me feed you."

"Thank you," Kyla replied, "but we can't. It would be too much of an imposition."

The woman dismissed her objection with a wave of her hand. "Nonsense. You are all welcome. My husband and I don't have much, but what we do have we are more than willing to share."

Kyla smiled. "That's a very kind offer," she replied. "We'd be honored."

The woman took Kyla's arm in hers. "Good," she said. "Come with me. By the way, my name is Perla."

"I'm Kyla. This is my partner, Matt, and our friend, Xiomara."

"Pleased to make your acquaintance," Perla said.

Kyla smiled. "Me too."

32

Mrs. Castillo

FOLLOWING THE ORDERS of his boss, Armando Canales, Rafael Cisneros arrived in the tiny fishing village of Puerto Lempira, parked his car in front of the pale yellow house with the grey tile roof, and observed the property for signs of activity. He opened his phone and took a quick look at the family photo of the man and his wife and daughter, which Canales had texted to him the previous evening. The woman was pretty, with porcelain skin and a bright, radiant smile. She appeared to be in her mid-thirties, their daughter eight or ten. In the photo, mother and child wore matching sundresses: yellow, with gaily painted sunflowers. The little girl sat on her father's lap, his arm around her waist. His wife stood behind them, her hand on her husband's shoulder. They were an attractive, happy-looking family. According to the information on the vehicle's registration, the family surname was Castillo, and this was their home address. He had not been provided the names of the man's wife and daughter, but that was unimportant. What was important was that they come with him when he asked them to. Logic dictated that Castillo's wife would not be prepared to go anywhere with a man she did not know and who appeared suddenly at her door, much less with her young daughter in tow. This was a not a problem. This wasn't his first time conducting a public abduction. The key wasn't just in the scripting of the event but more so in its execution. Only a handful of Armando's high-ranking clica members, such as himself, maintained a clean-cut, professional look. Rafael's appearance was far removed from the heavily tattooed and shirtless rank and file of MS-13 street soldiers and low-level thugs who made up the majority of the Mara Salvatrucha. The lightweight suit he wore fitted him well and showed off his muscular frame. His black leather shoes were polished to a fine shine.

If he had not been a member of one of the world's largest criminal organizations, he could have easily been taken for a New York City stockbroker.

Rafael opened the car's glove box, removed his handgun, slipped it into the cross-draw holster he wore beneath his jacket. Never before had he run into a situation where presenting the gun had been necessary to convince his abductee to comply with his demands and accompany him. In all likelihood, this assignment would be no different. Besides, he was armed with something much more powerful than a gun.

He carried a badge.

Rafael glanced at the house, saw movement behind the drapes.

Someone was home.

He opened the door of the unmarked black Dodge Charger police car, stepped outside, walked up the driveway, knocked on the door, stepped back, waited. Seconds later, the woman in the picture opened the door.

"Mrs. Castillo?" Rafael asked.

"Sí," the woman said. "I'm Ana Castillo. Can I help you?"

"Are you the wife of Xiomara Castillo?"

"I am," Ana replied. Concerned upon hearing the mention of her husband's name, she fully opened the door. "Why do you ask?"

Rafael slipped his hand into his jacket pocket, removed his fake credentials, presented them. "My name is Lieutenant Rafael Cisneros. I'm with the National Police. I'll have to ask you to come with me."

"Why?" Ana asked. "What's wrong?"

Rafael maintained a well-practiced, neutral expression. "There's been an accident," he lied.

Ana brought her hand to her face, covered her mouth. "Dear God. Is my husband...?"

"I'm sorry, Mrs. Castillo. I don't have the full details on your husband's status at the moment. He's been airlifted to El Alandra Hospital in Tegucigalpa. I've been instructed to drive you there. I recommend we leave as soon as possible."

"Yes, of course," Ana replied. Her voice was panic stricken. "My daughter..."

"Please try not to worry, Mrs. Castillo," Rafael said. "I know this must be very difficult for you. Take a moment to pack a few things for you and your daughter. Is she here?"

"Is who here?"

"Your daughter? Is she here or at school?"

"Amalia is here. I kept her home today. She's running a low fever."

"Is she well enough to travel?"

Ana nodded. "I think so."

"Good."

Ana opened the door. "I'll need a few minutes to get ready. Please, come in."

Rafael stepped into the modest home as Ana hurried down the hall and entered her daughter's bedroom. Rafael spied the woman's purse and car keys lying on a small wooden bench a few feet ahead. It seemed he had caught her as she was preparing to leave the house. He listened carefully, heard the child's objections to being forced to leave the comfort of her bed. He opened her purse, reached inside, retrieved her cell phone, powered it off, slipped it into his jacket pocket, then walked back to where he had been standing.

Ana and Amalia appeared a minute later. The little girl shuffled down the hall, rubbing her eyes, while her mother struggled with a shoulder bag she had haphazardly stuffed with their belongings.

Ana stopped suddenly. "Xiomara!" she said. "I didn't pack anything for him, just clothes and toiletries for Amalia and me."

Rafael shook his head. "Perhaps it's best if you deal with that later. The priority right now is getting you to your husband's bedside."

Ana nodded. "Of course."

As Ana reached for her purse and keys, Rafael picked them up. He slung her purse strap over his shoulder. "Your arms are full," he said. "I'll carry your purse to the car and lock your door."

Ana smiled. "Thank you."

Rafael nodded. "De nada."

At the police car, Rafael opened the rear door for Ana and Amalia. "I'm sorry," he said. "I know it's tight back there."

Ana smiled as she slipped inside. "We'll be fine."

Rafael walked to his door. Outside the car, he removed his phone, placed a call.

"Sí?"

"It's me," he said. "I have the wife and the daughter."

"Good," Armando replied. "Bring them to the warehouse."

"On my way," Rafael replied, then ended the call.

33

The Guy With The Gold

HANDS RAISED, WASHBURN called out to the bodyguard holding him and his partner at gunpoint outside the Lima Lounge. "I'm going to reach into my pocket and remove an envelope," he said. "It's for your boss, Juan Cabral."

"What's in it?" the bodyguard demanded. "Show me!"

Washburn carefully opened his jacket, removed the envelope, opened it, fanned the bills.

"Toss it to me," the bodyguard ordered.

Washburn shook his head. "I don't think so, pal."

"Then get back in your car and leave!"

"You sure Mr. Cabral would be happy with you getting between him and twenty grand in American cash? My guess is he'd have your head on a spike."

Washburn's remark caused the bodyguard to reconsider

his situation. The gun wavered in his hand. "What is your business with Mr. Cabral?"

"I have a proposition for him that's both urgent and financially luctrative. I need five minutes of his time. If he accepts my offer, great. If he doesn't, that's fine too. Either way, he keeps the twenty large, with no strings attached."

"Mr. Cabral's busy. He can't see you now."

"Didn't you hear what I just said?" Washburn dropped his arms. "Oh, fuck this," he muttered, then crossed the road.

The bodyguard reacted in an instant, took aim at the operative. "Stop!" he yelled.

Washburn said nothing, continued to advance on the man.

The bodyguard issued a second warning. "I said *stop!*"

Washburn walked up to the man, stopped when he was directly in front of him, then took another step forward. The muzzle of the bodyguard's gun pressed into his chest. He looked him square in the eyes.

"Listen, asshole," he said. "I know exactly who and what you are. You're paid muscle, a bullet stopper. Your job isn't to make decisions. It's to open and close the fucking car door while you pretend to pass yourself off as a tough guy to your boss who, by the way, really doesn't give two shits about you one way or the other and would replace you with the next loser dumb enough to step up to take your place faster than you can pull that trigger. But you want to know what your biggest problem is right now? It's not your boss. It's me. Why? Because I'm the guy with the gold. I'm the guy who can make your boss a hell of a lot richer in five minutes than he is already. Best of all, my money's squeaky clean. So do yourself a massive favor. Holster that gun, take this envelope, walk inside, give it to Cabral, tell him that I want a meeting, and that it would be unwise for him to make me wait a second longer than I already have. Think you can handle that, Sasquatch?"

The bodyguard stared at Washburn, returned his weapon to its holster, snatched the envelope out of Washburn's hand. "Wait here," he said.

"Make it fast," Washburn replied.

The second bodyguard kept his weapon trained on Washburn as his associate entered the nightclub.

Hobbs crossed the road, stood beside his partner. "Someone must be wearing his lucky underwear," he said.

"What do you mean?"

"That was a dice roll. How'd you know he wouldn't shoot you?"

"Would you have shot me if I told you I had twenty grand you needed to give to Ferriman?"

"Maybe."

"Really?"

"Accepting bribes is a violation of Agency policy."

"Which apparently, in your rule book, is punishable by death."

"I suppose you're right. Even Ferriman might consider that action a little extreme."

The nightclub door swung open. The bodyguard stepped out. "Mr. Cabral will see you now," he said. He held the door for the two operatives.

Washburn spoke as they entered the club. "See how easy that was?"

"Not so fast," the bodyguard said. He gestured with his fingers. Washburn and Hobbs knew what he was inferring. They raised their arms, allowed themselves to be patted down and their weapons confiscated. The bodyguard pocketed the guns. "You'll get them back when you leave," he said. "Follow me."

The three men crossed the dance floor, followed the bodyguard through a door marked PRIVATE, then ascended a staircase to the second floor. The bodyguard stopped outside an office at the end of the hallway, opened the door. "I have them for you, sir," he said.

Juan Cabral called out. "Gentlemen, please come in."

The bodyguard stepped aside, permitted Washburn and Hobbs to enter the office.

"Thank you for seeing us without an appointment, Señor Cabral," Washburn said.

Cabral stood from behind his desk, extended his hand. "It's not often I'm presented with such a gift before having even met my benefactor," he replied.

Washburn shook his hand. "My name is Andrew Washburn. This is my associate, James Hobbs. We were given your name by a reliable source and told you might be able to help us resolve an important matter as expeditiously as possible."

Cabral smiled. "And just who might this reliable source be?"

"Someone who would prefer that you know them for their deep pockets rather than their name."

"It's always a good rule to put a face to the money."

"I'm sure it is. But every rule has its exception. This is that rule."

Cabral nodded, motioned for the men to sit. "And why would I want to help the CIA?" he asked.

Washburn said nothing.

"Oh, come now," Cabral said. "Who else but the Agency

would know enough about me to have two of its operatives ask for a meeting out of the blue and have the financial means to drop twenty thousand dollars on my desk just for the privilege?"

Washburn realized there was no point in lying to Cabral. He nodded. "Two of our operatives are missing. We believe they have taken refuge in your country. My partner and I are under orders to return them to the United States to face disciplinary action. We're aware of how difficult that will be without local assistance. Considering the urgency of the matter, we thought it would be best to work with a local contractor, so to speak, who could help us expedite their recovery."

Cabral nodded. "I do have the connections to make that happen. Of course, you realize you're asking me to mobilize a small army on your behalf."

"I do."

"And that such a request comes at a price."

"Of course."

"Just how badly do you want your people back?"

"This matter is of the highest priority, Mr. Cabral," Washburn replied. "Read from that what you will."

"I see," Cabral replied. He leaned back in his chair, folded his arms. "Exactly how high a figure did you have in mind?"

"Why don't you tell me how much you think your services are worth and I'll tell you if you're even in the ball-park?" Washburn replied.

Cabral smiled. "This could be interesting."

Washburn pointed to the pen and notepad sitting on Cabral's desk. "Write down a figure. I'll let you know if it's doable or not. Just keep one thing in mind."

"What's that?"

"This is a one-shot deal."

Cabral nodded. "Fair enough." He picked up the pen, wrote down a number, folded the slip of paper, slid it across the desk.

Washburn retrieved it, read the note. "Done," he said.

Cabral smiled. "Very good. I'll provide you with my account number. As soon as the money has been deposited, I'll put out the word."

"Half now, half when they're in our custody," Washburn said. "And we need them alive. Not a scratch on them."

"Agreed," Cabral said. "You'll have your people back in no time. There's nowhere in Honduras they can hide where the Mara Salvatrucha won't be able to find them."

"Good." Washburn removed the ghost card from his pocket which Grace Poncaya had given him, placed a call, provided Cabral's banking information.

"You're all set," he said. "Check your account."

Cabral opened his computer, logged into his bank account, smiled. "Very good," he said. "Now, tell me. Who are we looking for?"

Washburn opened his cell phone, pulled up the agency pictures, showed them to Cabral. "His name is Matt Gamble. The woman is Kyla Reese."

Cabral nodded. "Send me their pictures. I'll get my men on it right away."

34

One More Day

OLEG ARRIVED AT the marina, parked his car in the main lot, removed his bags from the trunk, walked along the pier, boarded his boat, removed his keys.

John Simmons heard the approaching footsteps, emerged from his yacht's galley, a cup of coffee in hand. He called out to Oleg. "Well, look who's back."

Oleg unlocked the hatch, looked up. He could barely handle Simmons's superior attitude on the best of days, and the way this day had started had already left him feeling a little volatile. "What's that supposed to mean?" he quipped. "You keeping tabs on me or something?"

Simmons shook his head. "Me? Nah. The cops? Yep."

"The police came by?"

"I already told you, Schroeder. They want to talk with

you about what happened to our late friend, Earl. You know, the security guard who was killed."

Oleg opened the hatch. "Of course I know who Earl is, or rather, *was*," he replied. "When did they come by?"

"Yesterday around 7 P.M. They asked me if I'd seen you lately."

"And?"

"I told them no, that you keep odd hours."

"What kind of answer is that?"

"An honest one. Let's face it, you're not exactly a social butterfly. You never attend any club events or parties and keep pretty much to yourself."

"You have a problem with that?"

Simmons sipped his coffee. "Me? Nah. But other people do."

"Yeah? Like who?"

"Wendy Wigmore."

Oleg rolled his eyes. Wigmore, whose wife was a billionaire, was the club's self-appointed queen of all things social. The couple prided themselves on organizing and hosting the glitziest and most glamorous parties aboard their luxury yacht. Not to have been invited to a Wigmore function was the club's equivalent of being shunned. Oleg could tolerate the two women less than he could John Simmons. "Wendy Wigmore's Botox-enhanced lips can kiss my ass," he replied.

Simmons smiled. "Can I quote you on that?"

Oleg called out from inside the galley as he stored his belongings. "Chapter and verse."

"See, Schroeder? That's your problem. You don't know how to play the game."

Oleg ascended the galley stairs, stepped onto the deck.

"There's a difference between not knowing how to play and not wanting to, John."

"The Wigmore's are good people to know," Simmons replied. "Who knows? You might find yourself in a bind one day and need to call in a legal favor from a heavy hitter."

"I fight my own battles. I don't need anyone to do that for me, least of all the Wigmore's."

"You sure about that? You might be singing a different tune after the cops finish speaking with you."

"What are you not telling me, Simmons?"

Simmons shrugged. "Forget it. It's none of my business."

"You're gonna drop that on me and walk away?" Oleg asked. "I don't think so. Fess up."

Simmons sighed. "Okay, Schroeder. But I'm only telling you this because I like you."

"Yeah, right. What is it?"

"The cops were asking about an explosion that happened the other day. You know anything about it?"

Oleg felt his blood rush to his face. He hoped Simmons hadn't noticed his flushed reaction. "Explosion?"

Simmons nodded. "On the water, a few miles from here."

Oleg shook his head. "I'm not aware of one."

"Huh," Simmons said. "That's strange."

"What is?"

"Someone submitted a report to the Coast Guard. Said they thought it was your boat they saw blow up. Obviously, it wasn't."

"Why would they think it was my boat?"

"They thought they recognized it through their binoculars."

Oleg's throat went dry. He swallowed hard. "*Who* thought they recognized it?"

Simmons shrugged. "Don't know. Cops never mentioned a name. But I'll tell you this much."

"What?"

"They're pretty damn anxious to talk to you. If I were in your shoes, I'd call them. The sooner, the better."

Oleg nodded. "I'll do that."

"There was one more thing."

"Oh?"

"The guy who reported seeing your boat made it clear that he never saw its name on the transom. That it was the *Off The Hook* was just a guess."

"Then why would he think it was me?"

"Good question. Ask the cops. Maybe they'll tell you. Anyway, I've got to run. Wigmore's are hosting a party tonight on their yacht. I take it you won't be there?"

"And break a perfect non-attendance record?" Oleg replied. "I don't think so."

"Maybe you should reconsider, Schroeder. You look stressed. A couple glasses of wine might do you good, help you unwind."

"Personally, I'm more of a Scotch guy."

"Wine, Scotch, beer, name your poison. You can be sure the Wigmore's will have it."

"I'll think about it."

"Good enough," Simmons said. "Now, before you do anything else, call the cops. The other club members are already talking, and you know how finger-pointy some of them can be."

"Present company excepted."

Simmons smiled. "Of course."

"All right," Oleg said. "Thanks for the heads up."

"Don't mention it. Later."

John Simmons waved goodbye and descended the stairs into his galley.

Oleg did the same.

From the bar cabinet, he grabbed a glass and the bottle of Macallan, opened the bottle, poured himself a shot, downed it, then thought about what Simmons had told him.

Someone had seen the explosion, reported it to the authorities.

Maybe returning to the *Off The Hook* wasn't such a good idea after all.

The agents had told him to wait.

He would give them a day or two to come through with the money they had promised him. After that, five million or not, he would disappear.

He thought about the morning, the massage, the nightmare, and what it all meant.

Perhaps he should have flown to Switzerland after all.

35

A Few Enemies

MATT, KYLA, AND Xiomara followed Perla across the dirt road from the old double-wide trailer home which served as Rus Rus's hospital to her modest home. Inside, the living room featured a worn couch, two easy chairs, a small bookshelf crammed with paperback novels, and an old-fashioned tube television. Four white resin chairs were tucked neatly under a simple aluminum table in the dining room. A glass vase filled with colorful flowers adorned the table.

"My husband is in the bedroom," Perla said. "He'll be right out. Please, take a seat and rest while I prepare lunch."

"Can I help?" Kyla asked.

Perla shook her head. "No, my dear. You are my guests. All you have to do is make yourselves comfortable."

"Thank you, Perla," Kyla said. "You're very kind."

Perla smiled. "You're welcome."

From the hallway, Perla's husband entered the kitchen. He stopped when he saw the strangers.

Matt and Xiomara rose from their chairs to greet the man.

"Urbano, this is Kyla," Perla said. She pointed to the two men. "That is Matt and Xiomara. They'll be joining us for lunch."

Urbano stared at Kyla and Matt. "You're Americans," he said.

Matt nodded. "We are."

"Not me," Xiomara said. "I'm from Puerto Lempira."

"Xiomara drove us here," Matt said. "My friend, Kyla, stayed here many years ago. She came to visit a friend, but your wife informed her that he had been murdered."

Urbano stared at Kyla. "I think I remember you," he said. "You were with the men at the airstrip."

Kyla nodded. "I was."

"We were told very little about what was happening there," Urbano said, "only that it was a military operation of some kind. The National police made it very clear to us that we were to give your people any support you needed."

"I hope we weren't too intrusive," Kyla replied.

Urbano shrugged. "It wouldn't have mattered if you had been. When the National police order us to do something, we do it. Authority is not questioned here in Rus Rus."

Kyla recognized the man now. He was the elder who had meted out community justice against the young man who had been caught stealing and cut off the teen's hand with a machete while his parents looked on.

"The friend you're referring to who was murdered," Urbano said. "I take it you mean Alvaro Marroquin?"

Kyla nodded. "Yes."

Urbano shook his head. "His death was senseless," he said. "He should have known better."

"Known better?" Matt asked.

"Than to argue with a madman."

"Who are you referring to?"

"The one man in our region who everyone fears. Armando Canales."

Xiomara looked at Kyla. "That was who you spoke to on the phone," he said. "The man who threatened to kill you once he found you."

Urbano turned to Kyla. "*Found* you?" he asked. "Is Canales looking for you?"

"He might be," Kyla replied.

Urbano looked confused. "I don't understand."

"We had no intention of running into trouble with anyone," Matt interjected. "Kyla and I needed to leave the United States. She suggested we come to Rus Rus, that it was the quietest place she'd ever lived, so that's what we did. Unfortunately, things haven't gone according to plan."

"Is anyone after you besides Canales?" Urbano asked.

"We might have made a few enemies in the U.S. government."

"I take it by government enemies you're talking about the CIA?"

Matt and Kyla didn't reply.

"Please," Urbano said. "You don't think we can spot American operatives when we see them? The Central Intelligence Agency has been using our airstrip for the last twenty years, long before your wife arrived."

Matt shook his head. "Kyla's not my wi--"

"Your government has been good to us," Urbano continued. "The hospital across the street, basic though it might be, was built and staffed by American doctors and aid workers. Same for our general store. We may have very little, but what we do have is due to the support we have received from your country. If there's anything we can do to help you, we will."

"As a matter of fact, there is," Kyla said.

Urbano paused. "I'm listening."

"Tell us what you know about Armando Canales and where we can find him."

The aroma of sizzling ground beef and refried beans filled the kitchen. Perla removed warmed tortillas from the oven and set the table with plates and utensils, dishes of sour cream, pickled cabbage, rice, and fried plantain. "Armando Canales will have to wait," she said. "First, you eat."

36

Update

NA AND AMALIA sat in the cramped back seat of the unmarked Dodge Charger. The little girl squirmed in the tight space, tried to get comfortable, couldn't. Finally, she lay across the seat and placed her head on her mother's lap. Ana ran her hand over her daughter's forehead to soothe her. "It's okay, Mali," she said. "The lieutenant will get us to the hospital soon."

Rafael glanced in his rearview mirror at mother and daughter. "Is she okay?" he asked.

Ana nodded. "She's always fussy when she's not feeling well."

"I have a bottle of cold water you can give her if it will help," he offered.

Ana stared out the window as the police car raced along

the road. "She'll settle down in a few minutes," she replied. "Once she does, she'll fall asleep."

"All right," Rafael said. "It's here for you if you need it."

"Thank you."

"De nada."

"How long until we get there?" Ana asked.

"It's hard to say. The traffic in and around Tegucigalpa will start to pick up soon. That might slow us down a little."

"Can you turn on your siren and get us there faster?"

"It's not necessary," Rafael replied. He pointed to the service light bar mounted behind his windshield. "My lights are on and easily seen. Drivers tend to see them before they hear the siren."

Just as Rafael made the comment, Ana watched a distant car pull over to the side of the road, yielding to the police car, giving it plenty of room to pass.

"Besides," Rafael said. "Although the car's interior is soundproof, the siren can still be a little loud when it's on. Your daughter just fell asleep. It would be a shame to wake her."

Ana smiled. "That's very considerate of you," she said. "If you don't mind me asking, do you have children?"

Rafael nodded. "One. A boy. He's eight."

"Same age as my Amalia."

"Your daughter seems like a little angel," Rafael said. "My Ernesto is the total opposite. He's all boy. My wife and I can barely keep up with him."

"Oh well," Ana said. "One day we'll wish we could have these years back. Like they say, they're only young once."

"For me, once is enough."

A moment of silence passed. Ana glanced nervously around the back seat.

"Is everything all right?" Rafael asked.

"My purse. I don't have it."

"It's up here with me. I carried it to the car for you, remember?"

Ana sighed. "That's right," she said. "I forgot. Do you suppose you could pass it to me?"

Rafael shook his head. "I'm afraid I can't do that."

"Why not?" Ana asked.

"The panel between us has no integrated sliding window," Rafael explained. "The small holes in it permit airflow, but that's all. It can't be opened. It's been designed that way to maximize officer safety when transporting a prisoner."

"Can you at least pass me my cell phone?"

"Sorry."

Ana thought for a moment. "Can you call the hospital for me? I want to get an update on my husband's condition."

Rafael nodded. "Sure. I can do that."

"Oh, thank you," Ana said. "Thank you so much!"

Rafael looked down, removed his cell phone from its belt case, powered off the phone, raised it to his ear, faked the call.

Ana listened anxiously to the one-sided conversation.

"Thank you. I'll forward the information to Mrs. Castillo," Rafael said. He lowered the phone, powered it up, slipped it back into its case.

"What did they say?" Ana asked.

"Your husband is stable," Rafael lied. "It was touch-and-go for a while, but he pulled through. He's sleeping now and probably will be when we arrive. You should do the same. We still have a long drive ahead of us. It wouldn't hurt you to get a little rest."

"Perhaps you're right," Ana said. "Resting would have been impossible a few moments ago, but now that I know he's not in danger I don't feel quite so scared."

Rafael lied again. "They took down my number as I instructed them to do. I told them you were with me and that we're en route. If something comes up, they'll call me. Should that happen, I'll wake you right away."

Ana smiled. "Thank you, Lieutenant," she said. "I would appreciate that."

"My pleasure," Rafael said. He watched her in his rearview mirror as she leaned her head against the passenger window and closed her eyes. Minutes later, he heard her snoring lightly.

The warehouse and Armando Canales awaited their arrival.

37

Power

JUAN CABRAL ADDRESSED the two operatives seated across from him. "Tell me about the people you're looking for," he said. "What did they do that was serious enough to warrant the CIA launching an international manhunt to find them?"

Washburn smiled. "They stayed out past curfew," he replied. "We prefer our operatives come home when the streetlights come on."

"Surely you can provide me with a little insight," Cabral said. "After all, I'm sending my men after them. They should know who they're up against."

"All your men need to know is that these targets are highly trained and capable of defending themselves against multiple attackers under virtually any condition. When your men encounter them, instruct them to hold Gamble and Reese at gunpoint until we arrive."

Cabral laughed. "You make them sound like they're Hollywood action heroes, not run-of-the-mill CIA operatives."

"Trust me," Washburn replied. "There's nothing run-of-the-mill about Gamble and Reese. They're two of our best."

"With all due respect, Agent Washburn," Cabral said. "My men are quite capable of apprehending two lone Americans."

Washburn nodded. "Keep telling yourself that while you watch the body count rise."

Cabral composed a text. "And if your people refuse to surrender when ordered?"

"If your men are as competent as you say, they should be able to secure them without resorting to violence."

Cabral smiled. "I'll make them aware of your request. But do not expect them to come under fire and not retaliate."

Washburn nodded. "Understood."

Cabral finished writing the group message, sent it. "There," he said. "My clica's will respond to me shortly. Once they have acknowledged my order, they'll forward it to the people in their district. I was quite serious when I told you I have the power to mobilize a small army, Agent Washburn. You're about to see the result of that firsthand."

Washburn smiled. "It seems to me that kind of power could only be wielded by a member of the Council of Nine."

Cabral smiled coyly. "The Council of Nine? I've never heard of it."

"The Mara Salvatrucha's top brass. The architects of the organization. Its key decision makers."

"Sounds like a group that would possess great influence," Cabral replied. "If it indeed exists."

Washburn smiled. "Oh, it does. I had no idea until you sent that text that I was seated across from one of its members."

"What makes you say that?"

"You didn't require a superior's approval before executing our request. Only a top Council member would have the authority to do that."

"I've been given permission to make certain decisions without the need to go up the chain of command," Cabral replied.

"Does that permission include the right to deposit half a million dollars directly into your personal bank account?"

Cabral leaned back in his chair and smiled. "You're asking some very pointed questions, Agent Washburn."

Washburn grinned. "I thought we were just having a polite conversation."

Cabral nodded. "Perhaps it would be best if you changed the topic to something not so accusatory."

"Of course," Washburn said. "I apologize if I said anything that made you feel uncomfortable."

Cabral shook his head. "You didn't." His cell phone began to vibrate. He picked it up, checked the incoming texts.

"Are those the replies you've been waiting for?" Washburn asked.

Cabral nodded. "All but one have responded. He must be otherwise engaged at this moment. Not to worry. I should hear from him soon."

"Which means?"

"That your search is now officially underway. If all goes

as well, and I see no reason why it wouldn't, your operatives should be back in your custody by the end of the day, if not sooner."

"Very good," Washburn said.

"In the meantime, you and your partner must join me for lunch. The food here at the Lima Lounge is the best in Tegucigalpa. If you would prefer something which you don't see on the menu, please tell me. My chef will be happy to prepare it for you."

"Thank you, Señor Cabral," Washburn replied. "We'd be honored."

Cabral rose from his desk. "Excellent. Come. We'll dine in my private room."

Washburn and Hobbs followed their host out of his office, descended the staircase, crossed the dance floor, entered the private dining room, took their seats at the table.

Cabral checked his cell phone, smiled. "Forgive me," he said. "This could be important. I'll be back momentarily."

"Of course," Washburn said.

Together with his bodyguard, Cabral left the dining room. He spoke to the man. "Do you know if Armando Canales is ill?" he asked.

The bodyguard shook his head. "Not that I've heard."

"I've been trying to reach him. He hasn't responded to my text."

"Do you want me to look for him?"

Cabral shook his head. "I'm sure it's nothing. I'll wait until we've finished our meal. If I haven't heard from him by then, I want you to find him. When you do, tell him to report to me immediately."

The bodyguard nodded. "Yes, sir."

38

Durzuna

AMALIA STIRRED IN her mother's lap as the unmarked police car made a hard right turn and left the rural road. The girl sat up. "Mom," she said. "Where are we?"

Hearing her daughter's voice, Ana opened her eyes, lifted her head, looked out the window, read the large wooden sign as they drove past it. The words, weathered and barely legible, read **DURZUNA MILITARY DEPOT. AUTHORIZED PERSONNEL ONLY BEYOND THIS POINT.** She sat up, called out to Rafael. "Lieutenant?"

Rafael said nothing.

Ana called out again. "Lieutenant, why are we here? I thought you were taking us to Tegucigalpa."

"Sit back, Mrs. Castillo," Rafael replied.

Ana noted the sharp edge to his words. "What's going on?" she asked.

"You'll know soon enough."

"What are we doing here?" Ana asked. Fear crept into her voice. "Where is my husband?"

When Rafael failed to reply, Ana banged her fist on the plexiglass divider which separated them. "I demand to know what's going on!"

Amalia joined her mother, pounded on the divider. "Let us out of here!" she yelled. She checked her door for a lock release, found none, turned to her mother. "We're trapped, Mom," she said.

Rafael pointed to the man standing outside the decommissioned military supplies warehouse. "You're about to have all your questions answered."

Ana peered out the window. "Who is he?" she asked.

Rafael stopped the car in front of the warehouse, put it in Park, shut off the ignition. "The man who holds your lives in his hands," he answered.

"What are you talking about?" Ana pleaded. "I don't know him. What does he want with us?"

"You're about to find out," Rafael replied. He turned in his seat, looked over his shoulder. "I'm going to open your door now and let you out," he said. "I recommend that you don't try anything stupid." He pulled his gun from its holster, tapped the barrel against the plexiglass panel, got Amalia's attention. "And you, little lady. Don't even think about trying to run off into the rainforest. If my bullet doesn't kill you before you reach it, a million things in there will. Got it?"

The eight-year-old stared at the gun, then at Rafael. "Go screw yourself," she replied.

Rafael chuckled. He turned to Ana. "Your daughter's got quite a mouth on her, doesn't she?"

"She gets it from me," Ana replied.

"Good to know. But keep this in mind."

"What?" Ana asked.

"Between him and me, I'm the good guy. Now behave yourselves."

Rafael opened his door, stepped outside, walked over to his boss.

"Did they give you any trouble?" Armando asked.

Rafael shook his head.

"Good. Zip cuff them and bring them inside. Does the wife have her phone with her?"

Rafael nodded. He removed it from his jacket pocket, handed it to Armando. "I took it from her."

Armando slipped the cell phone into his back pocket. "I'm sure she's as anxious to talk to her husband as I am."

"Yes, sir."

Armando walked to the warehouse entrance, threw open the door, stepped inside.

Rafael returned to the police car, removed two sets of plastic zip cuffs from the trunk, closed it, then opened Ana's door. "Don't scream, don't kick, don't bite, don't fight," he said. "Just slide out of the back seat, stand up, turn around, and let me put these on. Resist me and you'll wish you hadn't. Understood?"

Ana nodded.

"Very good." Rafael motioned for her to exit the vehicle. "Let's go."

Ana followed his instructions, waited until the zip cuffs had been fastened around her wrists, then turned and faced her abductor.

"Not too tight, I hope?" Rafael asked.

Ana looked down, then up.

Rafael smiled. "Don't even think about trying to kick me in the balls and get away," he warned. "I've been doing this job a long time. You wouldn't be the first to have tried it and failed. That being said, if you're still thinking about it, I'll be happy to cuff your ankles together and let you hop your way inside, but I don't recommend it. These things tend to cut into the skin. So, what's it going to be? Cuffed feet or not?"

"Not," Ana replied.

"Wise choice."

Rafael moved Ana to the front of his unmarked cruiser. "Sit down, back against the bumper. Don't move." He walked to the back seat. 'Okay, kid. Your turn."

Amalia wriggled across the seat, exited the police car, stared at Rafael.

He paused, looked down at the girl, held out the plastic handcuffs. "Am I going to need to use these, or are you going to behave yourself?"

"I'll behave," Amalia said.

Rafael nodded. "All right. You heard the warning I gave to your mother. Same goes for you. Step out of line and you'll pay for it. Got it?"

"Yeah," Amalia said.

"Good."

Amalia walked to the front of the car, helped her mother to her feet. "You okay Mom?" she asked.

Ana nodded. "I'm fine, baby."

"Family reunion's over," Rafael said. He took the girl and her mother by the arm and walked them into the abandoned warehouse.

Armando Canales stood in the middle of the empty

floor, two folding metal chairs beside him. As his captives approached, he pointed. "Sit."

Ana and Amalia sat in the chairs.

"Who are you and what is this about?" Ana said. "Why are you doing this to us? We've done nothing to you."

Armando shook his head. "You're right. You haven't, but your husband has."

"Xiomara? My husband sells vegetables!"

"He's responsible for the deaths of eight of my men," Armando replied. "Perhaps not personally, but he played a part in their demise. Now he might very well play a part in yours." He removed his gold-plated handgun, walked behind Ana, dragged its barrel across her bare shoulders. The cold steel brushed against her skin, made her shudder. Armando moved to Amalia. Ana watched as he traced the weapon's muzzle down her cheek.

"Get that thing away from my daughter!" Ana yelled.

Amalia stayed calm.

Armando noted the little girl's cool composure. "You're much braver than your mother, aren't you?" he asked.

"I'm as brave as I need to be," she replied. "And much braver than you."

Armando smiled. "Is that so?"

Amalia nodded. "You're not brave. You're a coward. Only a coward would threaten someone with a gun."

Armando laughed. "Tell me, little one. Do you think your father is as brave as you are?"

"Braver."

"Really? Let's find out." From his jacket pocket, Armando retrieved Ana's cell phone, turned it on, pointed it at her face, unlocked it. He scrolled through her contacts, found Xiomara's name, placed a video call.

The phone began to ring.

39

Untouchable

MATT, KYLA, AND Xiomara enjoyed the company of Perla and Urbano Padillo and the wonderful lunch Perla had so kindly prepared for them.

Kyla turned to Perla. "I swear those were the best tortillas I have ever eaten, Perla. Thank you so much."

Perla smiled. "You're welcome, my dear," she replied. "Please, have another."

Kyla laughed. "No, thank you. I'm sure if I were to eat one more, I'll turn into a tortilla!"

Urbano agreed. "My wife is an amazing cook, isn't she?" He smiled and patted his generous belly. "I have the proof right here. See?"

Matt and Xiomara chuckled. "You're a lucky man, Urbano," Matt said.

Urbano reached across the table, took his wife's hand. "Yes, I certainly am."

Perla looked at Kyla, smiled. "Want to know the secret to a long and happy marriage?"

Kyla nodded. "Absolutely."

"Good food. Everything else is secondary."

Urbano looked at Kyla, winked. "I wouldn't say it's *everything*."

Perla pulled back her hand, slapped her husband on his shoulder. "That's enough of that," she teased.

Matt, Kyla, and Xiomara laughed.

"It must be nice living here," Kyla said. "It's so quiet and peaceful. Just you and nature."

"It used to be," Urbano said. "It's changing now."

"How so?" Matt asked.

"The gangs. They never bothered with unpopulated districts like ours before, but lately they've been making their presence known in and around Rus Rus. There are several grass airstrips and old buildings in the area, much like the one where Kyla was stationed when she was last here. At one time, they were routinely used by the U.S. military, but they've long since been decommissioned. It seems the gangs have discovered them and are restoring them for their use."

"For what purpose?" Xiomara asked.

"If I had to guess, I'd say it's to transport drugs, but I could be wrong." Urbano replied. "As far as I know, that's how these gangs make their money. Personally, I've never had an interest in investigating the facilities. That's a job for the National and Federal Police. Fighting the gangs is not a job for an overfed old man."

Kyla smiled. "Honestly, Mr. Padillo, you look like you

could hold your own just fine. You're a strong-looking man and, I might add, not that old looking."

Urbano winked at Matt. "You mind leaving her behind when you go? You can have her back when I'm dead."

Matt laughed. "Don't tempt her," he said. "She just might stay here for good!"

"We would be only too pleased to have her," Perla said. "And you."

"Thank you, Perla," Kyla said. "That's kind of you to say."

"Everyone in our village is getting old," Perla said. "We could use a young couple around here to liven up the place."

Kyla nodded. "Perla, would you mind telling me exactly what happened to my friend, Alvaro?" she asked.

Perla shook her head. "Poor Alvaro. His death was so unnecessary. He was only trying to protect his son as any father would have done."

"You said his death was drug-related?"

Perla nodded. "That's what we were told by his widow."

Urbano spoke. "The second we saw that fancy car of his drive into our village, we knew the devil had come to Rus Rus."

"You're referring to this Canales guy?" Matt asked.

Urbano nodded. "Si. El Diablo, the Devil."

Perla continued. "Somehow word had gotten back to El Diablo that Alvaro had said he would kill him if he ever saw him near his son Cesar again."

"How did Cesar end up on Canales radar?" Matt asked.

"He was an impetuous young man with a reputation for being violent," Perla explained. "Alvaro and Maria, his wife, were continually being called by his school. Cesar had been suspended several times for fighting and stealing the younger boys' lunch money."

"At knifepoint," Urbano added.

Perla nodded. "There was a rumor going around that he'd started a gang of his own and recruited several local boys into it. When Maria heard this, she gave him an ultimatum. He was to clean up his act or leave their house. Alvaro disagreed. He insisted the problem was not with Cesar but with the people he was associating with, that they were the ones who were encouraging him to make bad decisions. When he learned El Diablo had approached Cesar and asked him if he wanted to join his organization, he lost his mind. He became enraged, got his gun, and went looking for him. He returned home several hours later after not having found El Diablo. Maria said something changed in him that day. He had reached his breaking point. He would go for walks in the middle of the night. He wouldn't eat. He had become obsessed with finding El Diablo and killing him. Two days later, El Diablo showed up here. This time, the situation was reversed. El Diablo had come looking for Alvaro. He found him standing in his driveway. Maria said he got out of his car, took out his gun, walked up to Alvaro, and pressed it against his forehead. Alvaro didn't seem to care about the gun. He became enraged, yelled at him, told him what he thought of him, and that he had better pull the trigger because if he didn't, he'd never get the chance to do it again. Then he warned him to stay away from Cesar. According to Maria, those were the last words he ever spoke. When Cesar stepped out of his home to see who his father was yelling at, El Diablo pulled the trigger. Maria said he took aim at her too, but Cesar stepped between them. They talked for a few seconds, then Cesar got into El Diablo's car, and they drove away. Maria hasn't seen or heard from him since that day."

Kyla shook her head. "What a horrible ordeal to have gone through."

"I assume Maria called the police?" Matt asked.

"No, we did," Urbano said. "We heard the commotion and the gunshot that followed, then saw the car drive away. We were frightened. I told Perla to stay away from the window, that I would find out what had happened. When I felt it was safe to do so, I peeked out the window. That's when I saw Alvaro's body lying on the ground and Maria crying over him. We both ran to her. I tried to help Alvaro, but he was already gone. I called the police while Perla consoled Maria."

"What did the police do?" Kyla asked.

Urbano shook his head. "Nothing."

"*Nothing?*"

"I saw the look on their faces when I told them it was El Diablo who had killed Alvaro. I asked them what they were going to do about it."

"What did they say?" Matt asked.

"That they would report the incident and that a detective would be sent out to take our statements."

"And did they?"

Urbano shook his head. "An ambulance arrived an hour later and took away Alvaro's body. No detective ever showed up, and we know why."

"Because Canales has them on his payroll," Matt answered.

Urbano nodded. "He's a clica leader, a high-ranking member of the Mara Salvatrucha. He's untouchable, and he knows it."

Xiomara's phone rang. He looked at the screen and

smiled. "It's my wife," he said. "Excuse me for a moment. I need to take this."

Urbano smiled. "Of course."

Xiomara opened the video call, saw his wife's beautiful face. He smiled. "Hola preciosa," he said. "How's my—"

The image blurred as Ana's phone was quickly turned around. The face of Armando Canales stared back at Xiomara.

"Dios mio!" Xiomara said.

Matt looked up, saw the shocked look on Xiomara's face. "Xiomara," he asked. "You okay?"

"Do you know why I'm calling you on your wife's phone?" Canales asked.

Xiomara's mouth was too dry to respond. He swallowed, tried to speak, but could only shake his head.

Matt thought he recognized the man's voice, that he had heard it before but couldn't place it. Then it struck him. In the car. The man Kyla had spoken to on the cell phone he had taken from one of the gang members he had killed at the site of the fire. He snapped his fingers, got Kyla's attention, pointed to Xiomara, rose from his chair.

Xiomara's words came out as a whisper. "What do you want with my family?"

Canales turned the phone around to face Xiomara's wife and daughter. "What do you think I want with them?" he asked.

"Please," Xiomara said. "Don't hurt them. I'm begging you."

"What will happen to your family will depend upon your answer to my next question."

"What is that?" Xiomara asked.

"Where are the Americans?"

Matt and Kyla walked behind Xiomara, stepped into camera view. "We're right here," Matt said.

At the sound of Matt's voice, Canales turned the phone around. "You're the one who killed my men?" he asked.

"Actually, I prefer the word exterminated," Matt replied.

Kyla spoke. "He had help."

Canales smiled. "I know your voice. We spoke before."

"To be accurate, it was less of a conversation and more you threatening to kill me," Kyla replied. "Sorry, but I'm a stickler for detail."

"You're right," Canales replied. "So I did."

"Xiomara's family did nothing to you," Matt said. "They're civilians. It's us you want, not them."

Canales nodded. "You're right. I do."

"When and where?" Matt asked.

"Now," Canales replied. He directed his attention to Xiomara. "The abandoned military base in Durzuna. You know it?"

Xiomara nodded.

"Good. Be here in an hour. If you're one minute late, you'll be picking up pieces of your wife and daughter from here to Puerto Lempira. Do I make myself clear?"

Xiomara was too afraid to reply. He simply nodded.

Canales pointed the cell phone towards Amalia. "Say hello to your father."

Amalia stared into the camera. "Daddy!" she cried out. "Help ... *help!*"

Canales looked back into the camera. "One hour," he said, then terminated the call.

Xiomara stared at his phone, then fell to his knees.

40

Minutes To Live

JUAN CABRAL GLANCED at the waitress, called her over to his private dining table. The young woman hurried over. "Yes, sir?"

He turned to his guests. "Can I offer you gentlemen anything else? Perhaps a shot of tequila?"

Washburn shook his head. "No thank you, Señor Cabral."

"I take it everything was to your satisfaction?" Cabral asked.

Washburn wiped his mouth, set down his napkin. "Excellent," he replied.

"And you, Agent Hobbs?"

"Phenomenal," Hobbs replied. "That was the best steak I've ever had."

Cabral dismissed the waitress with a wave of his hand.

The woman took her leave. "Good," he replied. "It pleases me to hear that. I want my guests to be happy."

"You certainly accomplished that," Washburn said.

Cabral stared at his cell phone lying next to his plate, a look of concern on his face.

Washburn picked up on the sudden change in his demeanor. He pressed his host. "If you don't mind me saying so, you seem a little preoccupied. Is something wrong?"

Cabral smiled, shook his head. "I'm sure it's nothing."

"What's nothing?"

"I haven't heard from one of my men. It's out of character for him not to have replied to me by now."

"Perhaps you should try him again," Washburn suggested.

Cabral nodded, picked up his phone, placed the call.

Armando Canales answered the call. "Sí?"

"Where have you been?" Cabral asked sharply. "You didn't respond to my text. That was half an hour ago."

"I've had another matter to deal with."

"When I reach out to you, I expect you to put all other matters on hold. Am I understood?"

"Not this time."

Cabral's face flushed with anger. "What did you say?"

"I received your text. I chose not to respond."

"I assume you have a good reason?"

"I do."

"What is it?"

"You can call off the search. I've found the man and woman you're looking for."

"Excellent! Bring them to me."

"I can't do that."

"What do you mean, you can't?"

"All right. I won't."

"Are you out of your mind? Have you forgotten who you're speaking to?"

"No."

"You're disobeying a Council order."

"I am."

"Are you asking to be killed?"

"That's not my decision, is it?"

"Why are you putting yourself in this position, Armando? Are the Americans with you now?"

"No, but they soon will be."

Cabral let out a heavy sigh. "You've always been one of my most trusted men. Don't force me to make a decision I might later regret."

"They murdered eight of my men."

"What are you talking about?"

"I found their bodies. I was told it was the Americans who were responsible for their deaths. I won't let that go unpunished."

"I wasn't aware of that," Cabral replied. "I understand your anger and your desire for revenge, Armando. But you'll have to put those feelings aside. Retribution will have to wait. This matter is above you."

The line fell silent.

"Did you hear what I said?" Cabral asked.

"I did."

"I'm ordering you to stand down."

"I know."

"And?"

"Like I said, I won't do that."

Cabral opened a finder app on his phone, saw the pulsing blue dot that identified the location of Armando's phone, noted it. "I'm warning you, Armando," he said. "Should any harm come to the Americans by your hand, you will be dealt with in the worst possible way. Do you understand what I'm telling you?"

"I appreciate all you've done for me," Armando replied.

"Those sound like last words."

"They are."

"They don't have to be. Bring them to me. We'll forget this conversation ever took place."

"You and I both know that's not how this works. Goodbye, Señor Cabral."

Armando terminated the call.

Cabral stared at his phone in disbelief. Never before had anyone disobeyed a direct Council order, let alone a trusted clica leader.

Washburn spoke. "What was that all about?"

Cabral barked out an order to his bodyguards. The men rushed out the door, readied the car. "We need to leave," he said.

"Is there a problem?" Washburn asked.

"Nothing I can't deal with."

The operatives followed their host out the front door of the Lima Lounge to his car. "Where are we going?" Washburn asked.

"To my helipad at the airport."

"Why?"

"Your people are in danger," Cabral stated. "If I'm right, they may have only minutes to live."

The men jumped into the vehicle.

The Land Rover tore away from the curb, headed for the airport.

41

Caviar Taste

KYLA KNELT, HELD Xiomara. "It's going to be okay," she said. "Nothing is going to happen to your family. We'll see to that."

Xiomara shook his head. "You don't know Armando Canales like we do. He may have killed them already. He's ruthless, a monster. He doesn't make idle threats. If he said he'll kill them if we don't get to Durzuna within the hour, that's exactly what he'll do."

"Then we better get moving," Matt said. He shook hands with Perla and Urbano. "Thank you for everything," he said.

"Di nada," Perla replied.

"Buena suerte," Urbano said. "Godspeed."

Kyla helped Xiomara to his feet. "How far are we from Durzuna?"

Xiomara took a deep breath, steadied himself. "A little over an hour. We'll never make it in time."

"Yes, we will," Matt replied.

"How do figure that?" Kyla asked.

"You see what kind of car we're driving? It's a Trans Am. It's been modified, which means it's probably faster than anything on these roads. And with little to no police presence to be concerned about, we can drive as fast as we damn well want to, especially if I'm the one behind the wheel."

"You?" Xiomara exclaimed. "You don't even know where you're going!"

"No, but you do."

"What do you mean?"

"I'll drive while you navigate. If we run into trouble along the way, Kyla will take care of it."

"Meaning?"

"Meaning she'll blow whoever the hell gets in our way off the road."

Kyla smiled. "Sounds like I'm riding shotgun, literally."

Matt put out his hand. "Give me the keys."

Xiomara fished his hand into his pocket. "I'm not so sure I like this idea," he said.

"You have a better one?"

"No."

"I didn't think so. *Keys*."

"This is bad," Xiomara replied. "Really bad."

"It might seem that way to you," Kyla said, "but try not to worry. Matt and I train for this. It's what we do."

Xiomara dropped the car keys into Matt's hand. "All right," he said.

Matt hurried to the door. "Let's go."

As the trio reached the car, Matt called out to Kyla. "Check the trunk."

He jumped into the driver's seat, found the release lever, pulled it.

Kyla grabbed the lid as it popped open, looked inside the trunk, tossed a thick blanket aside, called out. "Jackpot."

"Thought so," Matt replied. "No self-respecting gang member would be caught dead without a trunk full of weapons."

"Copy that," Kyla said. She inspected the cache of weapons hidden in the trunk of the car. "I have to give these guys credit. They may be scumbags, but they have caviar taste when it comes to weapons. It's a gangbangers wet dream back here."

"Take your pick and get in," Matt said.

"I'm in a Heckler & Koch kind of mood today," Kyla said as she removed a HK416 assault rifle fitted with a sound suppressor from the trunk, inserted its magazine, then opened the door of the Trans Am and hopped into the back seat. "Open the sunroof. If we run into a problem, I'll need full access to the bad guys."

Matt and Xiomara both got in. Matt turned the key. The car roared to life.

Perla and Urbano waved goodbye as the Trans Am raced around the back of the hospital, turned onto Devil's Road, and headed for Durzuna.

Urbano put his arm around his wife as they watched them leave.

"Think they'll be okay?" Perla asked.

Urbano shrugged. "We can only pray that they will."

Perla nodded. "I'm going inside to light a candle."

"For their protection?"

"Yes."

"Good idea."

Together the elderly couple entered their humble home and closed the door. For the first time in as long as he could remember, Urbano locked it behind him.

42

Loyalty

CISNEROS STARED AT his boss. "Are you sure about this, Armando?" he asked. "No one has ever defied a direct order from Señor Cabral before."

"Cabral can go fuck himself," Armando replied. "Those men who died were more than street soldiers. They were my friends. I recruited them, trained them, brought them up in the organization. Now, thanks to the Americans, they're dead, and their families no longer have a provider. This goes beyond following orders. It's personal."

"Maybe we should end this now, kill the woman and her kid, and leave."

"No."

"Why not?"

"Because I want to see the look on the American's faces

when I pull the trigger. I want them to know that they are the ones who are responsible for the family's deaths."

The police lieutenant shook his head. "You're making a mistake."

Canales locked eyes with his enforcer. "If you don't have the stomach for this, perhaps you should leave."

"That has nothing to do with it," Cisneros replied. "It's you I'm concerned about. We both know Señor Cabral will not stand for this. I heard your conversation. He threatened to kill you if you didn't stand down. We both know that when he threatens someone, he follows through on it. You'll have to leave Honduras and go on the run, which will do you no good because the Mara Salvatrucha has clica's worldwide. Someone will find you. And when they do, they'll kill you."

Armando shrugged. "I chose this life. So did you. We both know no one gets out of it alive."

"But *you* could," Cisneros insisted. "You're not like the rest of us. Everyone in the organization knows you're Señor Cabral's designated successor. When he dies, you'll be appointed to the Council of Nine. You have nothing to lose and everything to gain by standing down. Perhaps you should ask yourself if this is really worth it."

Canales said nothing.

"You can still rectify this, Armando. Call Señor Cabral. Tell him that when the Americans arrive, we'll hold them for him."

Canales paced the warehouse floor, tapped his gun against his leg.

Cisneros called out. His voice echoed off the walls of the vacant building. "You know I'm right. Admit that you were out of line and made a mistake."

Canales stopped, looked up at the bank of dust-covered windows that ran the length of the warehouse, several of which were open, their glass panes broken, vandalized. "You're right," he said. "If there's one thing Cabral values more than anything else, it's loyalty."

Cisneros nodded. "Yes, he does."

Canales turned, raised his weapon. "As do I."

He pulled the trigger.

Ana and Amalia screamed as the policeman's body collapsed to the warehouse floor mere feet away from them. The man stared up at them, his eyes fixed and vacant, his final expression a death mask.

"Shut up!" Canales yelled. "Shut up, *shut up*, *SHUT UP!*"

Ana and Amalia muffled their cries. Ana took her daughter's hand, held it tight, yelled at Canales. "Why did you shoot him? You didn't have to do that!"

Armando hurried over to them, pressed the muzzle of his gun into Ana's forehead. "What did you say to me?"

Ana said nothing.

"That's what I thought," Armando said. He pointed his gun at Cisneros's corpse. "Let that be a lesson to you. Cross me and you'll die."

Ana found the courage to speak. "You're insane."

Armando shrugged. "Perhaps." He checked his watch. "Your husband better bring the Americans to me soon. If he doesn't, you'll find out just how insane I really am."

"Do yourself a favor," Amalia said.

Armando smiled. "What's that?"

"Leave before my dad gets here. Because when he does, he's gonna kick your ass."

"A vegetable vendor kick *my* ass?" Armando laughed. "I don't think so."

"You think you're tough, don't you?" Amalia pressed. "You're not." She pointed to the corpse lying beside her. "He was a coward. So are you."

Armando raised his gun, pointed it at the girl. "Be quiet."

Amalia smiled. "Or what, you'll shoot me? A lot of good I'll be to you if I'm dead."

Ana spoke. "That's enough, Amalia."

"You would be wise to heed your mother's advice," Armando said.

"Or not," Amalia replied.

Armando lowered his gun, grinned. "With a mouth like yours, you must cause your parents a lot of grief."

"I'm just getting started," Amalia replied.

A gentle breeze blew in through a broken window and carried on it the distant sound of car tires spinning on loose gravel. Armando had been to the warehouse many times and knew well the sounds of the area. A vehicle had left the main road and entered the private roadway. Seconds from now it would reach the warehouse.

He smiled at Amalia. "Well, well," he said. "Daddy's here."

43

Nothing To Worry About

THE EUROCOPTER EC155's mighty turbine engine whined impatiently outside its private hangar at Palmerola International Airport as it awaited the arrival of its passengers. Seconds later, the blacked out Land Rover cleared the main security gate and raced across the tarmac. The chopper's blades began to turn. The bodyguards exited the vehicle first, drew their weapons, and formed a defensive perimeter around the SUV. Satisfied their surroundings posed no threat to the car's occupants, the principal bodyguard waved at the vehicle. Together with Juan Cabral, Agents Washburn and Hobbs exited the car, jogged to the helicopter, and climbed aboard. The bodyguards followed, secured the cabin door, took their seats, strapped in.

Cabral retrieved his communications headset from the

hook above him, put it on, motioned for his guests to do the same. Washburn and Hobbs followed his lead. The sound of Cabral's voice crackled in their ears as he spoke to the pilot. "Take us to Durzuna," he demanded. "The abandoned military warehouse."

"Yes sir," the pilot replied.

"What's our ETA?"

"Twenty minutes."

"Can you get us there any faster?"

"I'll try, sir."

"Do that."

The chopper lifted off the ground, picked up speed. When it reached the required altitude, the pilot banked the machine sharply to the right and opened the throttle. The airport fell away from view as the helicopter raced towards Durzuna.

Washburn addressed Cabral. "What do you mean our people are in danger? You assured us that you had everything under control."

Cabral nodded. "I do."

"Doesn't sound like it to me."

"A minor problem has presented itself," Cabral confessed. "Don't worry. It's nothing that can't be dealt with quickly."

"But big enough for you to believe that Gamble and Reese may only have minutes to live."

"Like I said, it's nothing."

"Who were you talking to?"

"No one you need to concern yourself with."

"I have a million reasons that say otherwise."

"Are you threatening to withhold your payment to me?"

"I'm not threatening anything. I'm telling you straight

up. If anything happens to Gamble or Reese, our deal is flushed. You won't see another fucking dime. Do you understand me?"

"I don't appreciate your tone, Agent Washburn."

"Too fucking bad."

Seated across from the agents, listening to the conversation in their headsets, feeling the rising tension between the two men, the bodyguards slipped their hands under their jackets.

Washburn stared at them. "Don't even think about it," he said. "I guaranfuckingtee you that by the time you've pulled your weapons you'll both be dead."

The men ignored the agent's threat, stared at Cabral.

"Don't look at your boss," Washburn said. "I'm the one who'll be turning off your brain, not him."

Cabral met his men's gaze, shook his head.

The men removed their hands from their weapons, placed them in their lap.

"Smart move," Washburn said. He turned to Cabral. "Answer my question. Why are Gamble and Reese's lives in danger?"

Cabral sighed. "It seems they've been on quite a killing spree since they arrived in Honduras. A number of my men are dead, all of whom reported directly to my second in command."

"If Gamble and Reese killed your men, you can bet they had a damn good reason for doing so."

"That might be true, but it's irrelevant. You don't know this man like I do. If he's decided that they're to be held accountable for their actions, there'll be no changing his mind."

"I thought you were the man in charge, that your word was law."

"I am, and it is."

"Apparently not."

"This is a rather unusual situation, Agent Washburn. Never before in the history of the Council of Nine has a display of insubordination of this magnitude occurred."

"I don't give a rat's ass about the Council of Nine and its history," Washburn replied. "What I do care about is the safe return of our operatives. So, the question is, what are you going to do about it?"

Cabral removed his cell phone, placed a call.

"Ola, Señor Cabral."

"Listen to me carefully. I'm en route to the abandoned military base in Durzuna. Gather your men and go there. Find Canales and hold him until I arrive."

"Canales, sir?"

"Yes."

"May I ask what this is about?"

"No. Just do as I say."

"And if he refuses to listen?"

"You have my permission to wound him but do not kill him. He has much to answer for. I'll deal with him personally."

"Of course, Señor Cabral. We'll head there now."

"Good. I'm in the air, ten minutes out. Meet me there."

"Yes, sir."

Cabral terminated the call, turned to Washburn. "There," he said. "My men will take care of it. You have nothing more to worry about."

"Let's hope they do a better job of handling it than you have so far."

Cabral said nothing. He turned away from the CIA agent, stared out the window of the helicopter. Below, jungle treetops rushed past.

His mind was focused on Armando Canales, or more specifically, what he was going to do to him when at last they came face to face.

44

Helpless

THE TRANS AM fishtailed off the main road, then turned onto the broken asphalt pathway leading to the decommissioned military base. Matt hit the brakes, brought the vehicle to a sudden stop, turned to Xiomara. "How much further until we reach the warehouse?"

"This road zigzags for a thousand feet, then opens up to the main grounds," Xiomara said. "The warehouse is on the left."

"Accessibility?" Kyla asked.

"There's a main entrance door without a doorknob. Vandals broke it off years ago. Push on the door and you'll step right into the warehouse."

"What about the interior layout?" Matt asked. "Rooms, desks, tables, chairs?"

"A few rooms," Xiomara replied. "They used to have glassed-in walls, but they've long since been destroyed. Now it's just a big open space with graffiti-covered walls. When the military left, they took everything of value with them."

"You're telling me that once we're inside the building there's nothing available to use for cover if Canales starts shooting?"

"Correct."

Matt sighed. "Perfect."

"What about secondary entrances or exits?" Kyla asked. "There have to be fire doors of some kind. The military wouldn't construct a building without them."

Xiomara nodded. "There are. Two of them."

"Where are they located?"

"At either end of the building."

"Any cover opportunities there?"

Xiomara shook his head. "I don't know. It's been years since I've been here." He paused. "But one thing comes to mind."

"What's that?" Kyla asked.

"There's a catwalk that runs across the back of the building. It was used to clean the outside windows. There's a sister catwalk on the inside wall. If you can open a window without being heard, you'll be able to get into the building. You'll have a full line of sight from there."

Kyla threw open her door, stepped out of the car. "On it," she said. She slung the assault rifle across her back, ran up the road.

"Watch your six," Matt called out as he watched her disappear from sight.

Matt turned to Xiomara. "You ready?"

Xiomara nodded nervously. "I am."

"Good," Matt said. "Let's go."

He punched the accelerator.

The Trans Am raced ahead, reached the main compound. Outside the warehouse sat a white Mercedes and a second vehicle. Both were unoccupied.

"Let me guess," Matt said. "The Mercedes belongs to Canales."

Xiomara nodded.

"And the black town car?"

"That's an unmarked police car," Xiomara replied. "Do you think they've come for Ana and Amalia?"

Matt shook his head. "I doubt it. If that's a cop car, whoever's driving it isn't here to help your family. They're probably on Canales's payroll."

"Dear God."

Matt stepped out of the car, removed his gun, chambered a round, raised the weapon, followed its front sight toward the warehouse's steel entrance door, eased it open, peered inside. Xiomara followed close behind.

Sunlight illuminated the entranceway ahead of him, confirmed their arrival.

From inside the warehouse, a voice called out. "Do anything stupid and the woman and child die."

The element of surprise now lost to the traitorous beam of sunlight, Matt opened the door and walked into the warehouse with Xiomara at his side. He raised his hands.

Several feet away from Canales, a man lay motionless on the ground.

Canales yelled. "I know you're carrying. Lose the weapon."

Matt set his gun down on the concrete floor.

"Kick it over," Canales demanded.

"Do I have to?" Matt asked. "It's a nice gun. Leather grip, blue-steel barrel, good weight. It'd be a shame to scratch it up."

The sound of Canales chambering a round echoed throughout the building.

"Okay," Matt called out. "Point taken." He kicked the weapon, watched it slide across the floor. It stopped at Canales's feet.

Xiomara saw his wife and daughter sitting on the metal chairs beside the gang leader. The man's gun was pointed at Amalia's head. Xiomara panicked, began to run to them.

Matt called out. "Xiomara, wait!"

Canales raised his weapon, pointed it a foot away from the frightened father, fired. The round skipped off the floor.

Terrified at the prospect of being shot, Xiomara stopped in his tracks. Helpless, he stood in the middle of the warehouse, watching as his tiny family cowered and cried.

Canales motioned with his gun. "Both of you walk over here... slowly."

Matt reached Xiomara, put his hand on his shoulder. "You okay?" he whispered.

Xiomara nodded.

Matt could feel the man's body trembling under his touch. "Good," he said. "Now's not the time to lose it. You don't want to end up like that guy, right?"

Xiomara shook his head.

"All right," Matt said. "Stay with me."

Together they walked toward the gunman.

From outside the facility came the distinct thrum of helicopter rotors. A chopper was inbound, traveling low, approaching the warehouse at a high rate of speed.

The fragile windowpanes shook as the craft reached the building, then passed over it.

The unsecured steel door through which they had entered the facility blew open from the force of the down-draft produced by the chopper's mighty blades, sending a whirlwind of sand and debris rushing into the building and scurrying across the floor.

The helicopter was preparing to land.

45

Cover

THE HELICOPTER PILOT spoke into his microphone as he circled the warehouse, then held his position above the ground.

Cabral nodded at his bodyguards. The men opened the chopper's doors, drew their weapons, trained them on the warehouse entrance.

"If Canales steps outside and opens fire, kill him," Cabral ordered.

The senior bodyguard nodded. "Yes, sir."

Washburn and Hobbs stared down at the once vital compound, the asphalt of its broken grounds now over-grown with weeds and scattered with debris. Washburn spoke. "Any idea who the three cars belong to?"

"The white Mercedes is Armando's," Cabral replied. "As for the other two, I don't know."

A fourth vehicle suddenly entered the compound at speed.

"Your people?" Washburn asked.

Cabral nodded.

The agents watched as four men exited the car, retrieved their weapons, took cover behind the vehicle. One of the men looked up, signaled the chopper. Washburn recognized the hand sign. "He's telling us they'll provide cover fire if we need it. Tell your pilot to set down."

Cabral gave the order.

The helicopter began its descent, touched down near the abandoned warehouse.

The five men disembarked from the craft, kept low, spread out. Washburn and Hobbs ran to the side of the warehouse while Cabral and his bodyguards made their way to the men at the car.

Cabral spoke briefly to his men, then watched as they broke from cover and ran to the side of the building opposite the agents.

Washburn and Hobbs advanced along the wall until they reached the steel entrance door. Washburn raised his hand, made a fist. *Hold position.*

The leader of the four men nodded, waited.

Cabral followed his bodyguards to the door, called out. "Armando?"

No reply.

"Armando," Cabral continued. "It's Juan. I'm coming inside. I have men with me. Do not shoot. There are many of us. You won't stand a chance. The last thing I want is to see you get hurt. Call out if you can hear me." He waited for a reply. Seconds later, it came.

"You can come in," Canales yelled. "Everyone else stays outside."

Cabral's bodyguard whispered to his boss. "Sir, I can't let you do that. Canales could kill you the second you step inside the building."

Cabral shook his head. "He won't."

There was apprehension in the bodyguard's voice. "With all due respect, sir, you don't know that."

Cabral nodded. "Then do this. If you hear a gunshot after I walk through the door, breach the warehouse, and light him up. Otherwise, wait for my command."

The bodyguard reluctantly agreed. "Yes, sir."

Cabral opened the door, called out. "Armando, I'm coming in. I'm unarmed."

Armando replied. "Come to me. Slowly."

"As you wish."

Arms raised and weaponless, Juan Cabral entered the building.

46

A New Player

KYLA USED THE thunderous roar of the approaching helicopter to her advantage, moving quickly as it passed over the treetops under which she had taken cover, running from the tree line to the back of the warehouse, and climbing the rickety stairs to the dilapidated steel catwalk. From there, she peered in through the bank of broken windows, located Armando Canales standing beside the seated woman and her child, saw a body lying on the ground several yards away from the gunman. Matt and Xiomara stood near the dead man. The downdraft produced by the choppers' powerful rotors caused the weakened windows to shake in their frames. She watched as a distracted Canales looked up at the ceiling, then followed the path of the sound as it passed overhead and traveled beyond the opposite wall. She pushed hard on the window's broken latch, felt it give way, then climbed inside, lowered herself down to the inside catwalk, scurried along the structure, and positioned herself in a direct line of sight to the woman and her child. Camouflaged by the catwalk's steel grid and the darkness of the wall behind her, she lay prone, aligned the rifle, targeted Canales in the weapons sight piece, slipped her finger over the trigger, then waited for Matt to make his move. If Canales attempted to shoot Matt, Xiomara, or his family, she would squeeze the trigger, send a round downrange, and watch the bullet escort the sonofabitch straight to hell. When the warehouse door suddenly opened and a voice she did not recognize called out, she paused.

A new player had joined the game.

Hands raised, the stranger entered the building.

She listened as they talked.

"WHAT ARE YOU DOING, ARMANDO?" Juan Cabral asked. "Who are these people and why are you holding them prisoner?"

"The better question is what are *you* doing here?" Armando asked. "How did you find me?"

Cabral stepped further into the warehouse. "The wonders of modern technology," he replied. "Your cell phone's tracking app. I need to know my leader's location at all times, remember?"

Driven by his desire for revenge, Armando had completely forgotten about the agreement he had made with the Council of Nine to be tracked. "This has nothing to do with you, Juan," he said. "Leave now."

Cabral lowered his hands, took another step toward his second-in-command, shook his head. "I can't do that, Armando."

Armando pressed his gun against the back of Amalia's head. She whimpered.

"No!" Xiomara called out. "If you want to kill someone, kill me. Don't hurt my wife or daughter!"

"He's right, Armando," Cabral said. "I don't know who these people are or what they're doing here, but they're obviously civilians. We don't kill civilians, especially women and children. You know that."

Armando redirected his weapon away from Amalia, pointed it at Xiomara, yelled. "It's all his fault!"

"What are you talking about?" Cabral asked. He turned to Xiomara. "Who are you?" he asked.

Xiomara shook his head. "I'm nobody. I'm just a vegetable vendor. That's all."

"How did you get mixed up in this?" Cabral asked.

Matt spoke. "He's telling the truth. He played no part in your men losing their lives. That was all me."

"You and the bitch I spoke to on the phone," Armando said.

"Watch your mouth, asshole," Matt warned.

Armando swung the weapon toward Matt. "Before I kill you, I want to know why you killed my men."

Cabral stepped in front of Matt, blocked Armando's line of fire. "Listen to me, Armando," he said. "Under no circumstances is this man to be harmed. Do you understand?"

Armando couldn't believe what he was hearing. "Not harmed? What are you talking about?"

"Arrangements have been made which are of no concern to you," Cabral stated. "His life and that of his partner are of great importance to me. Neither of them is to be killed."

"Are you telling me you know who he is?" Armando asked.

"I do."

"And you're *protecting* him?"

Cabral nodded. "I am."

"Why?"

The warehouse door suddenly swung open. Cabral's men swarmed the facility, accompanied by Washburn and Hobbs. The men spread out, surrounded Armando.

"Drop your weapon!" Washburn yelled. "On the fucking ground! Do it now!"

Overwhelmed at being taken by surprise, Armando looked around the warehouse, stared at the armed men, then back at Cabral. "You won't do anything to avenge their deaths, will you?" he asked.

Cabral shook his head. "No, I won't. Now do as you've been told and drop the gun."

From the catwalk came a loud whistle.

Armando looked up, searched for the source of the sound.

Kyla called out, waved. "Up here, sweetheart. Peekaboo."

Armando felt the gravity of his situation. "So, this is what it comes down to," he said. He glared at Cabral. "I've given everything to the Mara Salvatrucha and the Council of Nine. This is what my loyalty is worth?"

"It's nothing personal, Armando," Cabral said. "It's strictly business."

Armando replied solemnly. "I understand."

"I knew you would," Cabral replied. "Now, please drop the gun."

Armando stared at his boss. "Do you know what the saddest thing in the world is?" he asked.

"Drop the gun, Armando," Cabral said firmly.

Armando shook his head. "To have lived a life that has been wasted, as mine has."

Cabral watched the gang leader level his weapon at him, then heard the eruption of gunfire as multiple rounds echoed off the walls of the empty warehouse.

Matt jumped forward, grabbed Xiomara and Cabral, pulled the two men to the ground.

Kyla watched Canales's body dance helplessly as round after round from his assailant's weapons penetrated his body. When the gunfire stopped, she sighted her weapon on the man's forehead, pulled the trigger, and watched his head explode. His lifeless body collapsed to the ground.

"That's for Alvaro," she said. She stood on the catwalk, called out to Matt. "You guys okay?"

As Xiomara ran into the arms of his wife and child, Matt helped Cabral to his feet and retrieved his weapon. "That depends." He turned to the men. "Are you the good guys or not?"

Washburn identified himself, pointed to his partner. "Washburn and Hobbs," he said. "We're here under orders from Director Ferriman. You and Reese are to accompany us back to the States to meet with Task Force Chief Cross."

"What about?" Matt asked.

Washburn shrugged. "Dunno. But if you're concerned about the capture/kill order issued against you, don't be. It's been rescinded."

Kyla called down to Matt. "You think what he's saying is legit? That it's over?"

Matt nodded. "Yeah, I do."

Kyla smiled. "You know, we could stay in Rus Rus a little while longer. Maybe catch a few rays, work on our tans."

"I have a feeling this might not be the best place for us to be right now," Matt replied.

"Copy that," Kyla said. She descended the catwalk staircase, walked over to Xiomara, Ana, and Amalia, removed her pocketknife, cut Ana free of the plastic zip cuff that bound her wrists. "Are you three okay?" she asked.

Xiomara nodded. "I have a lot to make up for, but yes, I think we are."

"Good," Kyla said. She knelt, took Amalia's hands in hers. "I'm sorry you had to witness that, honey," she said.

Amalia forced a smile. "It's all right," she said. "I'm fine."

Kyla winked. "Like father like daughter, right?"

Amalia looked at her father with pride. "You'd better believe it."

47

A Simple Trip

OUTSIDE THE WAREHOUSE, the chopper whined as the pilot brought the machine to life. The rotors slowly picked up speed. Before long, the helicopter was primed and ready to receive its passengers.

Cabral turned to his bodyguards and men. "I'm flying back to the hangar with my new friends. Drive the family home and dispose of the policeman's body and car."

"What about Armando?" a gang member asked.

"Leave him here. Put him behind the wheel and spray paint his Mercedes with gang markings. Make it look like he was assassinated by the Nicaraguans."

"Sí, Señor Cabral," the young man replied.

"And clean up the blood and shell casings inside the

warehouse," Cabral continued. "I don't want anyone to suspect anything happened in there."

Their tasks assigned, the gang members hurried to the warehouse to carry out their assignments.

ACROSS THE COMPOUND, Matt and Kyla spoke privately to Xiomara. Matt extended his hand. "Thank you for helping us, Xiomara," he said. "I'm sorry you and your family ended up in this situation. This was to have been a simple trip and nothing more."

Xiomara smiled. "I should have known it wasn't going to be an ordinary trip when you asked me what sort of weapons I could put my hands on."

Matt grinned. "I suppose you're right."

Kyla hugged the vegetable vendor, kissed him on his cheek. "You're a good man, Xiomara," she said. "You have a beautiful family. Take care of them."

Xiomara nodded. "They're all I live for."

Cabral's bodyguard approached the small group, spoke to Xiomara. "Are you and your family ready to leave?"

Xiomara smiled. "We are."

"Follow me," the bodyguard said.

Matt and Kyla watched Xiomara and his family climb into the Trans Am. Slowly, the car exited the abandoned military compound.

Cabral signaled the agents from the helicopter.

"Looks like it's time to leave," Matt said.

"Maybe not," Kyla said.

"What do you mean?"

"We could make a run for it and disappear into the jungle. What do you think?"

"The truth?"

"Of course."

"I think you're a glutton for punishment."

"And you're scared of a few spiders, snakes, and cats, aren't you?"

"If it lives in a jungle and has the ability to eat me alive, then yes... yes, I am."

Kyla took his arm in hers. "Okay, tough guy. Let's go for a ride."

Matt smiled. "Copy that."

48

A Gift For A Friend

JUAN CABRAL'S HELICOPTER touched down on the tarmac outside his private hangar at Palmerola International Airport. While in the air, Washburn had called ahead for the Agency jet to be rerouted from Tegucigalpa to the smaller, local facility. As the chopper's passengers departed the craft, the CIA's LearJet 75 taxied to their location. The pilot deployed the jet's airstairs and waited for the team to board.

"The transfer's been made," Washburn told Cabral as they exited the helicopter. The men concluded their business. "Check your account. It's all there, paid in full. One million dollars, as agreed upon."

Cabral opened his cell phone, logged into his banking app, checked his balance. He smiled. "It's always a pleasure doing business with the CIA."

"Let's not make a habit out of it," Washburn replied.

Cabral nodded. "I'm happy to have been of service."

"Believe me when I say this," Washburn replied. "If I'd had another option, I would have taken it."

Cabral smiled. "May I remind you that you reached out to me, not vice versa. Had you chosen to handle this extraction using your people and not mine, all of you would probably be dead by now. A team of Americans traveling unescorted through the most rural areas of Honduras is more than a recipe for disaster. It's tantamount to suicide. At some point you would have run into my men or those of my rivals. I assure you that would not have ended well."

Washburn allowed Cabral the last word. He extended his hand. "Thank you for your help."

Cabral shook the agent's hand. "Anytime. If you're ever back this way, be sure to visit. It would be my pleasure to treat you to another steak dinner."

Washburn smiled. He glanced at Hobbs, Matt, and Kyla. "You ready?"

"Just one last thing," Matt said. He gestured for the agent to join him away from the others where they could speak privately.

"What is it?" Washburn asked.

"One million dollars?" Matt asked. "That's how much you paid Cabral to find us?"

Washburn nodded. "Considering you and Agent Reese are standing here in front of me, I'd say it was money well spent."

"Then there's one more payment Uncle Sam needs to make," Matt said. "It happens, or Kyla and I don't set foot on the jet."

Washburn opened his jacket, displayed his gun. "You sure about that?"

Matt locked eyes with the agent. "Trust me, you'll be unconscious before your hand reaches the grip."

Washburn closed his jacket. "What do you mean, one more payment?"

"The man who helped us. Xiomara Castillo."

"What about him?"

"We both know his life is in danger now, as is his wife and daughter."

"Cabral's been paid, Gamble. It's over."

"Not for them it isn't."

"What do you want from me?"

"Give the Castillo's an opportunity to start over, to do wherever they want."

"How do you propose I do that?"

"The agency wouldn't have sent you down here and not provided you with a ghost card."

"So?"

"Break it out. Use it again."

"How much?"

"What do you care? Ghost funds are paid out through a sanctioned dark account. The agency doesn't give a damn how much money you spend to complete an assignment. You want us to get on the jet and accompany you home so that you can look like a hero to Ferriman, or not?"

Washburn sighed. "You're a real pain in my ass, you know that?"

Matt smiled. "I'll take that as a compliment."

"Don't."

"Take out the card and hand me your phone."

Washburn complied.

"Give me a minute," Matt said.

MATT DIALED THE LOCAL OPERATOR, got Xiomara's home number, called him.

"Hello?"

"Xiomara, it's Matt. Are you and your family okay?"

"Yes, Matt. Thank you for asking. How did you get my num—?"

"I only have a minute. I need something from you."

"Of course."

"Your banking information. I'm sending you a gift."

"Matt, you don't need to do that."

"Please, Xiomara. Your account number."

Xiomara paused, then provided Matt with the information he requested.

"Give me a few minutes, then check your account," Matt said. "Thank you again, my friend."

"You're welcome, Matt," Xiomara replied. "Goodbye."

MATT ENDED THE CALL, handed the phone back to Washburn. "I'm going to give you Mr. Castillo's banking information. You're going to call his bank and make a deposit."

"How much?"

"Our lives were worth a million dollars to the agency. Xiomara's family is worth at least that much to him. Make the call and deposit the money. One million. Not a penny less."

Washburn shook his head as he called the bank. "You know Gamble, I'm going to be happy as hell to have you out of my hair. I might even take a couple of weeks off to celebrate."

Matt smiled. "You do that."

XIOMARA PACED NERVOUSLY in his home office staring at his computer screen. What was Matt referring to when he said he would be sending him a gift? He refreshed his screen, then felt the blood drain out of his face as he looked at the updated balance in his bank account.

Matt had made a deposit all right.

One million U.S. dollars.

He called out to his wife. Ana entered the room.

Xiomara pointed at the screen, smiled. "Look!" he said.

Ana stared at the balance. "Is that *real*?" she asked.

Xiomara nodded. "It's for us. A gift from Matt."

Ana brought a hand to her mouth.

Xiomara reached out, took his wife in his arms, held her close.

In a moment of shared happiness, they wept.

MATT, Kyla, Washburn, and Hobbs boarded the LearJet 75, taxied down the runway. The jet took off, lifted into the air.

Soon they would be home.

Whether that would be a good thing for Matt and Kyla remained to be seen.

When they had left the United States, they had been

agency fugitives with an Alpha Level 1 capture/kill order issued against them. Now they were returning home, not as prisoners, but with a secret directive yet to be revealed.

Matt looked out the window as the Honduran coastline fell away, felt Kyla's hand slip reassuringly into his.

One way or another, they would face whatever lay ahead together.

They slept.

49

"You've Got My Number."

"I SHOULD HAVE flown to Switzerland when I had the chance," Oleg Schroeder said as he stared into the *Hook's* bathroom mirror and scratched the stubble on his face. He'd never had a problem growing a full, thick beard and was always surprised at how fast it would come in when he'd let it. The look suited him, or so he thought. It gave him a rugged, seafarer's look which he believed helped him sell his fishing charter services to his clients. He turned his head left, then right, examined the look even closer. "Damn, you're handsome," he said. "I think I'll keep this for a while, see how well it goes over with the ladies." He checked his watch as he exited the bathroom. It was morning. The half bottle of Macallan he had self-medicated with the night before to put him to sleep had done its job but left him with a hangover. He opened the galley blinds and winced as the harsh sunlight temporarily blinded him. Outside the boat, he heard noises on the dock. He dressed quickly, slipped on his deck shoes, baseball cap, and sunglasses, then unlocked the hatch and ascended the stairs to the deck.

John Simmons stood on the deck of his yacht, power washer in hand, spraying down the surface. He called out to his slip neighbor.

"Morning, Schroeder."

Oleg gave him a quick wave. If there were two things he didn't like, it was dealing with a morning hangover before a few cups of black coffee had done their job to alleviate the discomfort and a morning how-do-you-do with John Simmons.

"John," he replied.

"You missed one hell of a party last night," Simmons said.

"Party?"

"On the Wigmore's yacht. They really outdid themselves this time. Even had a midnight fireworks display. It was epic."

"Yeah, I'm sure it was."

Annoyed at Oleg's disinterested attitude, Simmons turned off the power washer. "What is the matter with you, man? You think you're better than the rest of us or something? You're always being invited to these blowouts, yet you never attend."

"I like my space, Simmons," Oleg replied. "You know that. I've only told you a million times." God, he needed a coffee.

Simmons pressed. "If you like your space so much, what

the hell are you doing here? You know this is the hottest marina in the city, right? We've got an applicant waiting list a mile long. Someone pretty much has to die before a spot opens up, and first shot at those go to surviving family members. The least you could do is show your face around here once in a while and let people know you even give a shit."

Oleg suddenly found himself overcome by a moment of self-reflection. He stared at Simmons, thought about his response before replying. He had all the money he would ever need and properties around the world under various aliases. *Did he really need another five million from the CIA?*

"You know what, Simmons?" he asked.

"What?"

"You're right."

Simmons stared at him. He was expecting a confrontational response, was ready for it. Schroeder's answer caught him by surprise. "I am?" he said.

"Yeah, you are."

Feeling empowered, Simmons puffed his chest. "Well, of course I am!" he barked.

"Give me a second," Oleg said.

Simmons waited as Oleg disappeared below deck, then returned a minute later. He dropped a large duffel bag at his feet. His backpack was slung over his shoulder. He walked to the back of the boat, removed the FOR SALE sign from the deck railing, tossed it into the galley, then locked up the boat.

"What are you doing?" Simmons asked.

Oleg smiled. "Something I should have done a long time ago."

"Oh yeah? What's that?"

"Leave this city."

"You're going? Just like that?"

Oleg nodded. "I need you to do me an important favor. Think you can handle it?"

"Depends. If you're gonna ask me to help you bury a body, that's not happening."

Oleg tossed him the keys to *Off The Hook*. "I want you to give those to someone. Tell him they're from me."

Simmons caught the keys, stared at them, then back at Oleg. "Who?"

"Earl the security guard has a son. He told me how much his boy loves the water and hopes to have his own boat one day. Now, he's got one. I don't know how old Earl's kid is. He might not even be old enough to operate the *Hook* yet. But at least she'll be here waiting for him when he is. I'll keep up the payments on the slip, so that won't be a concern. The boy just lost his father, John. He could use a little direction in his life. You and the other club members could give him that, but that's up to you. If you don't want to do it, toss back the keys. I'll give them to someone who will."

"This is one hell of a thing you're doing, Schroeder," Simmons said. "You sure about this?"

Oleg nodded. "Yeah, I'm sure."

"Okay. I'll see to it that Earl's boy gets the keys."

"Good. I'll take care of any ownership transfer paperwork that needs to be completed when I hear from you. You have my number."

"I do."

Oleg wrangled his belongings, stepped off the *Hook*, took one last look at his boat. "Take good care of your new owner, baby," he said. "He's gonna need it."

As he walked along the pier toward the parking lot, Oleg

felt Simmons staring at him. Without looking back, he raised his hand, gave him the finger.

From the deck of his yacht, Oleg heard Simmons laugh and call out.

"Right back at ya, Schroeder!"

50

NOMAD

C ENTRAL INTELLIGENCE AGENCY
Langley, Virginia

UNSURE OF HIS FATE, Matt waited nervously in the outer office. After five tense minutes, the phone rang on the executive assistant's desk. She took the call, spoke quietly, hung up, looked at Matt, and smiled. "Task Force Chief Cross will see you now," she said.

"Thank you, ma'am," Matt replied. He stood, opened the frosted glass doors which bore the logo of the Central Intelligence Agency, entered the office.

Cross sat behind his desk. "Agent Gamble," he said. "Please take a seat."

Matt sat, said nothing.

"Nice to see you made it back here in one piece," Cross said. "Which, judging by the after action report I just read, you and Agent Reese managed to do by the skin of your teeth."

"Permission to speak frankly, sir?" Matt asked.

Cross leaned back in his chair. "Go ahead."

"What exactly am I doing here? Last I heard, you wanted me put down. Agent Reese, too. You even sent Badger to terminate us, which didn't work out well for him."

"You disobeyed a direct order, Gamble," Cross replied. "You had to know there would be repercussions."

"There's no way that I was going to murder a man in front of his son."

"That wasn't your call to make."

"The hell it wasn't. It was my op. I was the one looking downrange, not Ferriman."

"He had eyes on the target just like you did."

"From the sky maybe, but not from my vantage point. I told him there would be another time to take out Gutierrez. I was prepared to go mobile and follow him, but Ferriman never gave me the chance. He was over-focused. I wasn't. Do you want to know why I accompanied Agent Reese to Honduras in the first place?"

Cross was not expecting that question. "Why?"

"To finish what I started," Matt said. "To take out the target in his own backyard and clear my name. If you wish, I'm still prepared to do that. Put me on a plane. I'll head back there and see that it gets done."

"You're a determined man, aren't you Agent Gamble?"

"I've never turned my back on an assignment before, sir."

Cross tapped his fingers on a dossier on his desk. "I know that. Your work in the field speaks for itself."

"Do I have your permission to terminate Gutierrez?"

Cross shook his head. "That won't be necessary."

"Why not?"

"The Gutierrez problem has taken care of itself. He died two weeks ago. Car crash. Ironically, his family was in the vehicle with him. They perished in the accident."

Matt was silent.

"That's not why you're here, Gamble. There's a reason why I rescinded the Alpha 1 capture/kill order against you and Agent Reese."

"Why is that sir?"

"Because you are the best operative in this agency. To have terminated you would have been a colossal mistake. I'm glad we were able to stop the clock before it ran out."

"That makes two of us."

"I have an opportunity for you, Matt. But know that if you accept it there'll be no turning back."

"I'm listening."

"There have been a number of closed-door discussions recently pertaining to the agency's need to establish an elite team, one which operates deeper in the shadows than we do now. We haven't acted on it yet because we've been waiting for the right candidate to present themself, someone whom we feel would be capable of heading up such an operation. We believe that individual is you."

"Me, sir?"

"That's right. You'll report directly to me and no one else. This is a black ops team, which means you'll be operating outside of the law and without agency support. You'll have everything you'll need and more. The scope of your assignments will be international. You and your people will be expected to pick up and go anywhere, anytime. Furthermore, your identities will be wiped clean. There's one more thing you need to know, Matt."

"Sir?"

"If you accept this assignment, your world will change forever. There will be no turning back. We've selected a name for the program which we feel best reflects that level of risk: NOMAD."

"Nomad?"

"**N**on **O**fficial **M**ission **A**sset **D**eployment. Everything you and your NOMAD team does will be off the books."

"Who exactly comprises this team?"

"That will be up to you. You'll have carte blanche to recruit whomever you want. Just keep the team tight." Cross stood. "So, what do you say, Matt? Did we make the right decision by offering this to you?"

Matt stood. "Yes, sir, you did."

Cross nodded. "Good."

"So what happens now?" Matt asked.

"You have three months to select your personnel and report back to me," Cross replied. "After that, you'll receive your first mission, and your team will go live." He picked up a sealed envelope from his desk, handed it to Matt. "Your security clearance has been raised. Everything you need to know about the program is in here. Read it, then burn it."

The envelope read, **OPERATION NOMAD. CONFIDENTIAL. EYES ONLY.**

"It's good to have you aboard, Matt," Cross said.

Matt nodded. "Good to be aboard, sir."

Cross took his seat. "That will be all."

Matt turned and left the Task Force Chief's office.

He had a team to recruit.

And ninety days in which to do it.

ALSO BY GARY WINSTON BROWN

MATT GAMBLE ACTION THRILLER SERIES

Good As Dead (Book 1)

Devil's Road (Book 2)

NOMAD (Book 3)

JORDAN QUEST FBI PSYCHIC THRILLER SERIES

Intruders (Book 1)

The Sin Keeper (Book 2)

Mr. Grimm (Book 3)

Nine Lives (Book 4)

Live To Tell (Book 5)

Nemesis (Book 6)

Tiny Bones (Book 7)

Old Ghosts (Book 8)

The Bad Man (Book 9)

Two Graves (coming soon)

Jordan Quest Digital Boxset 1 (Intruders, The Sin Keeper, Mr. Grimm)

Jordan Quest Digital Boxset 2 (Nine Lives, Live To Tell, Nemesis)

Jordan Quest Digital Boxset 3 (Tiny Bones, Old Ghosts, The Bad Man)

STANDALONE THRILLERS

The Vanishing

ABOUT THE AUTHOR

Gary Winston Brown is the author of the Jordan Quest FBI Psychic Thriller series and Matt Gamble Action Thriller series. He lives just outside Toronto, Canada.

If you enjoyed reading **DEVIL'S ROAD**, kindly rate and review it on Amazon!

JOIN GARY'S READERS CLUB

Want to be kept up to date on new release and preorder announcements, special offers (like signed paperback draws), and more ? It's easy. Visit my website to subscribe to my no-spam-ever newsletter and receive a free book!

GaryWinstonBrown.com

You can unsubscribe at any time, but I hope you'll stick around.

Printed in Dunstable, United Kingdom